BILLOUGHB

Lost Souls

D M Roberts

Billoughby 3
Lost Souls
By
D M Roberts

Copyright D M Roberts 2021

Acknowledgements

I would like to add a special thanks to all that have supported me in my books. Knowing that you have gotten as much from the characters' stories makes it worth writing them on their continued journey.

Table of contents

One

"I really do have to go soon."

Elsbeth looked up at Tom, her eyes as clear as the blue sky itself.

"A little while longer. Mary won't miss you for a few more minutes, surely?"

"Tom Billoughby you are a terrible young man. You will have Mary sending out the constabulary if you're not careful."

"Wouldn't it be funny if Father turned up looking for you?"

"It most certainly would not."

She smiled her soft warm smile, the one which made his smitten heart skip a beat.

"Could be worse."

"How so?"

"It could be my Mother,"

Tom replied as he stood and stretched in the hot rays of the sun.

Elsbeth scrambled to her feet, smoothing down the hems of her yellow cotton skirts.

"Oh Tom, don't. I positively dread what your Mother would make of all this."

Tom frowned, his youthful smile disappearing from view.

"They will understand, they have to. I do wish you would let me tell them. I want to shout it up to the Almighty himself. love you."

"We cannot."

"Why not?"

"Because I am so much older than you are. Because they expect you to meet a girl of your age and have children someday. Because your Mother is a dear friend."

"Then what am I?"

Elsbeth shrugged, he could see this wasn't an argument he was going to win, for now at least.

"You know you are very dear to me Tom, you make me happier than any woman deserves to be but, at what price?"

"I will not let this go, nor you, not for anyone. We can talk about it another time. Let's get you back home before they do send a search party out for you." He kissed her gently.

"Thank you, Tom."

Mary walked along the hall again, now and then she stopped at a room and peered in. Her eyes searching around.

"David. David if you are in here please come out." She called into the empty rooms.

"Do you think he's hiding Miss Mary?"

"He must be dear. Still, he's going to miss out on his meal if he doesn't come out soon."

The little girl nodded up at the woman.

"Anything?" Called Sally up the stairs.

"No, I can't find him up here."

Mary and Doris came into the kitchen.

"Here you are my little treasure, sit yourself down and tuck in."

Doris picked her spoon up and began to eat as the two women chatted behind her.

"I've looked around the building outside, not a sign of the little lad."

"Did you check in the stables?"

"I did, twice. I wandered down to the kitchen garden, I know he's a one for the carrots down there, not a whiff of him."

"Elsbeth will be back soon, what am I going to tell her?"

The unmistakable sound of the boy's voice came echoing through from the hallway.

"I only wanted to see the new piglets."

"That is all well and good young man but you must never go off on your own like that again. Miss Mary must be half out of her mind with worry."

"Miss Mary is more than half out of her mind. Where on earth did you find him?"

"Sitting on the fence down by the pigs."

"Wash your hands, David, we shall talk about this later." David skulked off to the pantry to wash his hands, mumbling about the injustice of grown-ups and their rules.

"I'm so sorry Elsbeth, one minute he was there, turned my back to help Doris and he vanished." Elsbeth laid her bonnet on the table.

"No harm done Mary, he's a quick one I'll give him that. I think I shall have to speak quite firmly to David this afternoon with regards to the dangers of going off alone."

She smiled at Doris who was busy finishing off her meal.

"Do you have any ideas, my sweet little girl?" Doris cocked her head to one side.

"No puddings."

"What a jolly good idea. We all know how much young Master David loves his puddings."

"That's not fair! I only went for a walk." He protested.

"We shall talk about it later David, come along, eat your food."

Grace wandered around the cottage. The boys were certainly doing a grand job of getting it repaired. Pulling out the ball of string from her bag she stopped at the window.

"Cate, be a dear and hold this for me." Cate obligingly caught hold of the other end.

"It won't be long now Ma."

"No, I think a few more weeks and they'll be done with the roof. Let us hope the weather holds long enough to get it finished."

"Don't let the farmers hear you say that. Tom reckons if we don't get some rain soon there won't be anything to harvest."

"Yes, it's been a tough old time for Robert this year. Mind, he's luckier than some. Mr Nash was telling me that some have had their fields ablaze in the heat, my heart does go out to them." Cate passed the string back to Grace.

"I know it's rattled the little one, she's barely slept."

"That brings me to another matter. Why don't you and Adam have a night out together, I can have the little one? I can't remember the last time you both went out on your own."

Cate smiled fondly at the older woman.

"Would you do that for us?"

"Of course I would, she's my granddaughter."

"I shall speak to Adam. Maybe we could get Tom along, the Thompson girl is old enough now to go out with an escort and it would do him good, especially after the news about Connie and that chap."

Grace thought for a while before speaking.

"I'll speak with Mrs Thompson when I call past. It would do him good, he's been ever so quiet of late."

"That's settled then. Oh, I am looking forward to it, maybe we could go dancing. Adam and I loved dancing when we were back in Ireland. He's ever so good you know."

"Like his father no doubt. Mr Billoughby is wonderful on the floor." Cate looked at the woman's face, she had a look that was far away yet content.

"Right, that's all we can do here for today." Grace wound the string up carefully as she made her way to the front door.

There was nobody more surprised than Tom when Grace told him of the plans to go out dancing.

"But Tom, we have already invited her, you can't let the poor girl down now. It's only for an evening, you don't have to marry her." Tom knew he wasn't going to get out of this one easily.

"You could have asked me first is all I'm saying. I barely know the girl. I could have someone, you didn't ask." Grace was perplexed. This was not like her easy going son at all.

"Have you someone?" "That's not the point Ma." Billoughby looked on as his wife tried to make sense of their usually placid son's reaction.

"It's one night son, do it for your mother, eh."

Tom left the room shaking his head. What was he going to tell Elsbeth? This is why he wanted the world to know, things like this just wouldn't happen if their secret was told. Throwing himself down on his bed he fell asleep quickly.

"Shall I wake Tom for supper?"

"I'd leave him for now my love. My he took on so didn't he?"

"I don't know what's going on in that head of his at the moment really, I don't."

"It might be this heat, gets to us all."

"No, I think it's something more than that."

"He has been working hard these past weeks, the lad's likely tired then we go offering him up for dancing with a miss he hardly knows."

Grace couldn't help feeling it was more than that. Still, nothing she could do about it for now.

Mary returned home tired that evening. Robert was waiting, a mug of tea in hand for his new wife.

"Hello my love, here, I made you a drink." Mary took the mug gratefully, she was parched after her walk.

"I don't know why you don't let me come to fetch you."

"You have more than enough to do without stopping to fetch me. How was your day?" Robert waited until his wife sat down, she looked weary today. Standing behind her he rubbed her shoulders as he spoke.

"Most of the day we have spent going back and forth from the stream. I don't know Mary if this hot weather keeps up. I haven't even started on the new house, what you must think of me." Mary looked up at her husband.

"I told you dear, I love the house as it is and see no reason to build another. There is more than enough space for us, goodness, we could fit another family in here with us and still have room to spare." This was one of the qualities he loved about Mary, she never complained, would happily make do wherever she could.

"Will the farm be alright?" Robert dragged the chair from under the table, it scraped across the stone floor. Taking Mary's hands in his he smiled.

"It will be fine my love, of that I am sure. Yes, we're luckier than most around these parts and no mistake." She nodded, it was going around the village at some pace that so many of the farmers were suffering far worse fates than they were. If things came to a crunch at least Robert and herself were financially quite sound, some were not as fortunate.

"Is there anything we can do to help the neighbouring farms do you think?"

"Short of making it rain my dear I imagine it will be a wait, and see what the rest of September brings." "Hmm, I was thinking more on a practical level."

"We can offer, proud lot us farmers." Mary spooned out potatoes as they talked, Robert sliced the cold pie placing a piece each on the plates.

"How about you my love. What have you been occupying yourself with today?"

Mary grimaced.

"Young Master David took himself off for a walk today. I searched every inch of the hall for him, thankfully he came back around two as Elsbeth was returning." Robert's ears pricked up. He shook his head, ridiculous thought.

"Where had he been. I imagine it was quite upsetting."

"He went to see the piglets. Yes, it was, he's still such a little fella that doesn't understand the world."

"Maybe we could have him here for a few days, I expect he gets quite bored of all the womenfolk in the hall." Mary couldn't help thinking this might be a wonderful idea for the youngster.

"You wouldn't mind that?"

"Not a bit, we'll make a farmer out of the little urchin yet."

"I shall speak with Elsbeth about it, I'm sure she will agree it's a splendid idea." The pair ate their supper, each with thoughts of their own on David, and the suffering farmers.

It was Saturday afternoon, Tom and Adam had been working tirelessly on the thatched roof.

"I think that about does it." Called Adam as he secured the last spar. The young men stood back as they admired their work.

"It looks so much better."

"It sure does. I reckon we deserve an evening out after this lot. Cate tells me that the Thompson girl is very much looking forward to dancing with you brother." Adam playfully ruffled his brother's hair.

"Get off you daft bugger."

"Are you excited? It's been a while since you courted a girl." Tom screwed his face up.

"I have no intentions of courting the girl, it's one night, no more than that."

"You never know, you might hit it off. Give her a chance eh Tom." Tom had no plans to give her a chance, he had found the woman for him.

"Alright lads."

"Hello Father, come to admire our handy work?" Billoughby stared up at the roof, stroking his chin as he walked around the cottage.

"You leaving that up there?" He nodded to the shirt that rested on the chimney stack.

"Oh Lord, I forgot about that." Adam scurried up the ladder to retrieve his discarded shirt.

"You walk back with me son. I imagine you'll want to make yourself all smart for the young miss."

"Why is it everyone is so set on me and this girl?" replied Tom haughtily.

"Calm down son, I didn't mean anything by it." Tom strode off in the opposite direction.

"Where are you going son. Tom, Tom come on back." Tom wasn't listening, he still hadn't had a chance to tell Elsbeth about the plans that had been made behind his back. He must put that right today before the village gossip did.

Elsbeth opened the door. Her face flushed when she saw a perspiring Tom standing there.

"Whatever is the matter?" she whispered.

"I had to come to see you." They could hear the sound of steps coming through the large hall.

"Go to the stables, I'll be there in a few moments." She asked in a hushed voice.

"Is everything okay dear?" It was Sally.

"Yes thank you, Sally. I thought I heard the door knocker."

"Probably those village children up to no good, thank goodness the weekends are only two days long."

"Yes indeed." Elsbeth made her way through the kitchens and out into the stable yards. She looked behind to make sure Sally hadn't followed her out, she hadn't.

"Tom." She whispered into the darkened building. "Over here."

"What is so urgent?" Tom stared down at his feet. He wasn't at all sure how Elsbeth would take his confession. "Tom?"

"I had to tell you. Cate and Mother have arranged for me to go out tonight with Mrs Thompson's daughter, I don't want to but it appears they have set the thing up and I can't get out of it. I did not want you to hear it from anyone else because it is not what it seems." Elsbeth smiled at the flustered beautiful face before her.

"Oh Tom, you should go. You should have a wonderful time and you mustn't give me a second thought." Tom was confused. Why would she say that? She was his every thought, surely by now she knew this.

"It won't change what we have between us?"

"We are lonely souls my dear Tom, should either of us find a more suitable companion I hardly feel it for the other to deny us that."

Tom stumbled back, he felt that a large fist had caught him right in the middle of his chest.

"Elsbeth?"

"You are young my dear, we knew this may happen. Go, have a good time. I'm sure the young lady will be entranced by you." Elsbeth stroked his face and smiled, turning away she left the building. She walked quickly back to the hall, trying hard to keep the tears from spilling onto her cheeks until she had at least reached the privacy of her room. Tom stood for a long while in the stables. What had just happened he wasn't sure, all he knew was he would not be dismissed that easily. Yes, he would go on this damned evening jaunt with his brother, however, he would return to his Elsbeth come the morning time. With that in mind, he headed off home.

Esther, Mrs Thompsons daughter, was a pleasant enough girl. She smiled politely when the trio arrived to pick her up.

"Look after my girl Tom Billoughby, you hear?" Called Mr Thompson as the door closed.

"Don't pay any mind to Father, he doesn't often allow me out on my own."

"You're in safe hands with us. Besides, we are only going to the Inn." Reassured Cate. Adam nudged Tom's arm.

"Say something to her." He whispered to his brother. Tom scowled, it was not a thing he was accustomed to doing but of late he found himself doing so, nonetheless.

"It was good of you to make up the four Miss. Thompson."

"Please call me Esther. It was good of you to ask."

"I didn't, it was my mother's idea." Tom instantly pressed his hand over his mouth, did he say that aloud?

"Regardless, it will make a pleasant change of company." Replied the undeterred girl. Cate shook her head. What had they done? Tom was quite obviously not comfortable with the arrangement and was making that most obvious. This was going to be a long evening! It was. Tom was solemn in his company and it did not go unnoticed by the young lady. Cate and Adam got up to dance to the tune played by Molly on the piano in the corner.

"I know you would rather be somewhere else." She finally said.

"Really. Whatever makes you say that?" "You have said nothing to either myself or them all the time we have been here." Tom looked into his mug of ale, he felt embarrassed that he couldn't hide his feelings more easily.

"I am sorry to have spoilt your night. I was asked you see, I was told of the arrangement not a day ago."

"That's quite alright. Shall we at least try to pretend we're having a good time? Come on, let's have a dance." Esther held her hand toward him, he hesitated then stood.

"I don't suppose it will hurt none." He muttered as they joined the others.

"Evening Tom." It was Robert, great that was all he needed.

"Robert."

"Miss. Thompson. Nice to see you young ens having a good time. Don't tire him too much mind, we have a busy week ahead of us." Esther laughed.

"No chance of that Sir." The evening proceeded to be a salvaged one with plenty of ale and dancing. Molly looked over at the young group smiling to herself. It had been a long time since the small Inn had played music, she was pleased that Cate had cajoled her into it.

The door to the Inn flew open, Molly ceased playing the piano.

"We need people to help us search the area. It appears the youngster from the hall has gone missing." Cried the Reverend Moore. His face was red with the heat and his rush to get there. Robert was first to offer his help, quickly followed by Albert and the 2 brothers.

"Tom, you escort the ladies home and meet us back here." Ordered Robert.

"Come on ladies, let's be quick about it." Cate and Esther collected their shawls and left with Tom.

"Thank you, Tom. Please be careful."

"I will Cate, see if Pa is in there will you?" Grace came to the door.

"What's happened?"

"Young David has gone missing by all accounts. We're getting the villagers together, those that can help, to look for him."

"I'll fetch your Father." Within minutes Billoughby appeared at the door with his hat on.

"Meeting at the Inn I hear son?"

"Yes, Pa. I will take Miss. Thompson home and meet you there."

"See you soon, my love," Billoughby called back to Grace.

"Be careful dear, you're still convalescing." Billoughby headed off in the direction of the Inn as Tom and Esther made for the Thompson's home.

"I can go by myself, Tom." She offered.

"Your father would have my hide, Miss. Thompson." She grumbled back.

"It's Esther." Tom wasn't listening, all he could think about was how his poor Elsbeth must be feeling right now. They arrived at the cottage to be met by Esther's Father.

"I heard, you get yourself inside my girl and I'll go with Tom." The two men walked briskly to the Inn, no words passed between them which suited Tom fine. Inside Robert and Billoughby were instructing the now packed room, who was going where and what time to meet back at the Inn.

Mary had her arm around Elsbeth.

"Stop blaming yourself, he'll be fine, you'll see. Get a sharp tongue from me when he gets back and that's no lie."

"I put him to bed as normal and he seemed alright. Why would he do this Mary? Is he not happy here?"

"Of course he's happy. Why wouldn't he be? He has more than likely wandered a bit too far, I bet he's curled up somewhere fast asleep right now." Mary hoped with all her might that this was the case. She continued.

"The men are starting a search for the young fella, you'll see, he will be back before the morning." Elsbeth sighed, she knew that Mary was probably right, and yet there was something, a feeling that the woman could not shake off.

"I'll make us a pot of tea. It's going to be a long night."

The two women sat and drank their tea in the parlour, the house seemed strangely quiet for the first time in a long time. Eventually, Elsbeth's head dropped to one side as she succumbed to sleep. Mary placed a shawl over the woman. The newly married woman was also harbouring thoughts of what might be. David would no more get up and leave the house in the dark any more than she would. Something was not right. Thankfully, the two younger girls remained asleep and, undisturbed, that in itself was a blessing. Soon, along wither sister-in-law, Mary was asleep.

Two

The sun was vaguely making its appearance behind a stray cloud when the door knocker jolted the two women awake. Mary scrambled to her feet, the incident of the day before forced its way to the forefront of her mind.

"I'll go." She said as she left the still confused Elsbeth to gather her thoughts.

"Good morning dear wanted to give you an update. We've found nothing as yet." Robert looked tired and weary as he rubbed his eyes.

"Oh no. Come in, my love and I'll make you some breakfast. We can't have you falling ill." She kissed her husband tenderly on the cheek as Elsbeth joined them in the hallway.

"He will be okay won't he?" Robert tried to put on a brave face, a weak smile appearing on his lips.

"Of course he will Miss. The lad's hiding, that's all."

Elsbeth knew that he was trying to be positive for her benefit.

"Yes, he's a devil for playing tricks that one." The three made their way to the cool kitchen. Mary began to fill the kettle, her mind racing with 'what ifs' she had grown quite attached to the children over the months they had been at the Hall.

"I shall check on the children." Elsbeth left the pair, climbing the staircase to the bedrooms.

"Be honest. Do you think something has happened to David?" Robert shook his head.

"It's hard to say, Mary, there was no sight, nor sound of him. We all took a section each, not one of us found anything." The whistle from the boiling kettle screeched through the air almost as a warning. The man ate quickly, stopping only to drink down his hot mug of tea. Elsbeth returned, baby in arms.

"I think we might have disturbed this little one." She kissed the child tenderly on her forehead, Dolly, wriggled impatiently in the woman's arms.

"Would you like me to take her, dear?" Mary didn't wait for an answer, instead, she plucked the warm infant from her sister-in-law's hands.

"You are so toasty warm, little one." She coed.

"I best be away, back to the farm Mary."

"Thank you, my love. You were a great help, mind you get some sleep and I will see you soon." Robert stroked Dolly's head as he leant in to kiss his wife goodbye.

"Not much chance of that, it'll be a quick chat with the lads then back out to search some more."

"Do be careful, Robert." Robert nodded to Elsbeth as he strode from the kitchen. The morning was still, other than the occasional sounds of wakening birds in the distance, no familiar sounds of David's feet running down the stairs came now as the women sat in silence.

Billoughby scratched his head. A habit he was prone to when he had a problem to solve.

"You'll wear a patch into your scalp if you don't stop that."

"I don't get it, Gracie."

"What don't you get dear?"

"Why, or even how the lad would simply disappear like that. It doesn't make sense. I've seen him around in the village a fair few times, he was happy there up at the Hall."

Grace knew this to be true, if ever there was a child content with his little lot in life it was David. It was a blessing the weather was as hot as it had been the woman thought, Grace could not bear to imagine the poor little fella out there somewhere in the cold night.

"We will find him, my love. Remember when Adam hid in the old barn? Must have been six or seven at the time. Half out of our minds we were, found him fast asleep in the hay." Grace laughed to herself as she recalled the sight of their son all those years ago.

"I do remember that. I wanted to give him a telling off, instead, I hugged him 'til he nearly popped."

The pair sat drinking their morning tea in quiet contemplation.

"Best get started back out there. Are you going to be alright here my love?"

"I will. Don't you go tiring yourself out my love, you barely slept last night. I thought I might go over to the Hall, see if I can lend a hand with anything." Billoughby nodded.

"Might be useful if the lads had a bite to eat in between searches." Grace hoped that it wouldn't come to another full day before David was found. It made sense to be prepared all the same.

"That's settled then. If you could set me down over at the Hall on your way." Grace tidied away the tea things, she was not one to leave a cluttered table even when she had things on her mind.

"Ready my love?" Billoughby was standing at the kitchen door, hat in hand.

"Cate. Cate dear."

"Yes, Ma."

"We're off to the Hall now dear, I don't know what time we'll be back. If you could sort yourselves out for lunch, possibly supper too."

Cate appeared at the living room door.

"You're not to fret over us Ma, we can manage just fine so we can. I pray the boy comes back soon."

"He will dear. Take care."

The morning was hot, as it had been every morning for the last few months. Billoughby steadied the cart as they turned into the courtyard of the Hall. Elsbeth was on the steps to greet them.

"Anything. I suppose it's too early in the day to ask. Would you like tea, I'm sure Mary has one on the go?"

"Nothing yet Mrs Stanhope. I won't stop thank you, we thought Grace might help you out today."

"That's so very kind of you Grace, I don't know whether I'm coming or going at the moment. Mary is making sandwiches in the kitchen. Sally is tending to the girls bless them. I am quite sure they know something is amiss." Tipping his hat, the Inspector left the ladies and set off to the meeting point at the Inn.

"Now dear, what can I do to help?"

The kitchen table was covered in prepared snacks along with jugs containing fresh water.

"My, you have been busy Miss Mary. Let me know where I can assist you." Mary smiled gratefully.

"It's so good of you Grace if you're happy to pull the trays from the oven, there's a thick towel over on the sideboard. That would be a help. I'm sure I've done too many rolls but it is so charitable of the men to search for our young David. I don't know what else to do." Mary struggled to bite back the tears. She had grown fond of the young fella, more so than the girls if she was honest. He had a heart of gold, but Lord was he a funny character. Sometimes, he knew exactly how to wrap Mary around his little finger, never with malice. Grace pushed a hanky into Mary's hand on her way to the oven. Saying nothing, for she was well aware this was a woman that would not be made a fuss of.

The Inn was open, unusual for this time of the morning. Billoughby pushed through the throng of men, he noticed Adam and Tom were already there. They were going over the areas they had covered the previous night.

"Morning lads. Any luck out there?" Tom shook his head.

"We tried all the places we would have hidden as youngsters Pa, not a sign of the little fella." Dragging out a chair with his foot, Adam nodded to his father to sit.

"I'm beginning to get a feeling. Keep it under your hats boys, no good upsetting anyone if we don't have to. I hate to say it but we could be looking at a snatching." Adam's eyes grew wide, he was a new father and the very idea of there being a person snatching children in the area made his blood run cold.

"Are you serious?"

"Can't see any other reason for it son. The lad went to bed as normal, a bit disgruntled by all accounts over a silly telling off. Nothing he hasn't had in the past mind, nothing that would have the lad run away that's for certain."

"Where do we start, if it is a snatching." Asked Tom. Tom could not imagine a stranger wandering around in his Elsbeth's home with him not there to protect her.

"First thing to do I suppose, would be to talk to them up at the hall. Find out if they had anyone wandering around over there that they didn't recognise, or did for that matter. Plenty of workers outdoors,

I'm sure they will have spotted any comings and goings over the last week or so. Had Miss Mary still been there the dogs would have alerted them?" Tom was beginning to feel uneasy, he had been there not 24 hours since and with no good reason he could give. Not to his parents. How was he ever going to explain that away? Billoughby continued.

"Let's hope he has tucked himself up somewhere for a quiet sleep." The sons nodded.

"We're going to do the fields next, with the haystacks up everywhere there's no saying he's not hiding amongst them. Eh, Tom?" Tom was on his feet.

"We'll get started then. If we find anything where will you be?"

"Most likely the Hall, I think it best to speak to people now, in case things slip their minds. When you need to eat they have prepared food over there, could you let the fella's know?"

"Will do Pa." Tom, Adam and a handful of the younger men made their way out of the Inn The Inspector shouted for everyone's attention.

"Right lads, Robert's good wife has laid food on at the hall so when you're in need head over there. The younger men have gone to search the fields, I suggest we sort into groups of 4 or 5 and start on the wooded areas. Any items that you come across that you might think of interest, keep hold of them and I'll collect them from you at the Hall. Any questions?"

"What if we, you know, erm, find something other than items."

"Good God Fred, what kind of thing is that to say?"

It was a reasonable question, one that had to be asked.

"Fred is right to ask, we don't know what has happened to now. Anything of that like, and I can't stress this enough, do not touch, do not cover with a coat or shirt. Have someone stay to make sure nothing gets disturbed but you must come to find me straight away as a matter of urgency. I'm hoping there won't be an incident of that sort, never can tell."

"Do you think he's okay? The little fella." Tom had been preoccupied with his thoughts, what would he say when questioned, he surely would be questioned of that he had no doubt. His father was thorough in his job, he would never shy away from Tom merely because he was his son.

"I hope so. It's going to be another scorcher, don't fancy the idea of him out in this heat with no water."

"No, me neither. I bet they are out of their minds at the Hall." Adam nodded, he couldn't imagine how he would feel if it were his child out there alone. Like the people of the village, he had come to think of the three as Mrs Stanhope's children. They hadn't been there a long time it was true, they had endeared themselves to all that encountered them.

"Over here." Called Ed. Tom, Adam and Jimmy raced off to where Ed was standing.

"What you found there Ed?" Ed was peering at a piece of torn striped cloth that had been tied loosely on a branch at the edge of the field.

"Looks like a bit of old rag that's got caught up, nothing to get concerned about." Ed shook his head.

"Look, see it's tied. My old mam gave the Lady at the Hall some nightshirts for the nippers that looked just like this. I ain't never seen a piece of cloth tied in a knot like that by the wind."

"No, that's been left by someone. See, torn in a straight line an all."

"I'll go back and fetch Pa. I don't think we're supposed to move it." Adam made back for the Hall as the trio left behind talked of what a clever sod young David was if it was he that left the clue.

"Miss Mary reckons he has quite a brain on his shoulders. Talks his way out of most things she reckons."

It was true, not only did David have an extremely inquisitive mind, he had a logic beyond his years for things that a child that age did not normally possess.

Billoughby arrived soon enough, Elsbeth sat alongside him in the cart. As soon as her eyes took in the cloth hanging from the branch she let out a scream. It wasn't a high pitched scream that one would have expected, it was a pained, hoarse scream.

"You recognise this?"

"Yes, it's from the nightshirt he was wearing only last night."

"Now Mrs Stanhope, try not to get yourself too worked up. This is a good sign is it not, means the lad is still well enough to think straight."

"Why would anyone do this Inspector? He's just a boy."

"Now, now. We don't know what has happened, don't let your imagination get you carried away."

That said, Billoughby knew in his mind that the lad would never have left this if things had been as they should have. No, this was most definitely foul play of some sort.

"Did you fella's look any further through the opening there?"

"No Pa, we thought it best to wait for you."

"Well done. Right I suggest we go carefully and follow the track. Jimmy, Ed you go that way. Adam and I will take this side. Tom, could you take Mrs Stanhope back over to the Hall, no point you hanging around here Miss in this heat."

"I would rather stay Inspector if it's all the same."

"It would be better if you didn't, I'm sure the little Miss's are upset with all the toing and froing, might be better for them if you keep things as settled as you can. Don't worry, if we find anything, you will be the first to hear."

Tom helped the reluctant Elsbeth into the cart, gently squeezing her hand as he did so, much to his surprise she pulled her hand from his. She was upset, it was obvious this had shaken her. The ride back was quiet, too quiet, eventually, Tom pulled the cart over to one side in the secluded lane.

"Why are we stopping?"

"He will be okay, David."

"You don't know that Mister Billoughby, nobody does or can. Maybe if I had not gone off in the afternoon I would have spotted something, anything to stop this from happening. I was selfish to the children, only thinking of myself."

Tom was still digesting the 'Mister Billoughby' it seemed stuck in his throat, he swallowed and yet it wouldn't go down.

"That's a silly thing to say, you have dedicated yourself to the children from the minute they came to you. You also are entitled to a life Elsbeth, you cannot blame yourself for something out of your control."

"I chose my life, they are my life now. Ride on please." Tom did as he was asked, there seemed little point in arguing the rights and wrongs with his passenger in her current state of mind. They arrived back at the Hall, Elsbeth alighted the cart before Tom could assist.

"What did they find?" It was Mary that came out to meet them.

"Oh, Mary, a piece of young Master David's nightshirt. What on earth has happened to our boy?" Elsbeth sobbed onto her sister-in-law's shoulders, Tom could only watch with aching helplessness for the woman he loved.

"Come inside dear, things will come right, you'll see. Tom, take some food back for the fella's if you will, you will find it in the kitchen." Tom sensed he was being dismissed as he made his way around to the kitchens at the back of the house. Placing his sack on the table he slowly loaded bread, ham and water into it.

"Hello." He turned to see little Doris standing in the corner. She was clutching a ragdoll that wore the same dress as she did.

"Hello, little Miss. Is that your dolly? She's as pretty as a picture."

"Miss. Mary made her for me. Did you find my David?" Tom felt his chest tighten as the piercing eyes stared beseechingly up at him. He tried to answer, his throat seeming to close at the leaving only enough of a gap for a croak to escape. Doris was stood beside him now, she tugged at his trouser leg.

"You can't find him?" Tom shook his head.

"You will." Her angelic face smiled up at him, she skipped out of the room grasping her dolly.

"Did you get what you need Tom?" Mary had watched the conversation from the doorway. Tom held the sack up to her, why couldn't he speak! Bloody hell, she must think him a fool.

"Taken us all a bit out of sorts, you get off now lad and try not to fret so, he will come home."

Back at the woods, they had found nothing tangible in Tom's absence, a few bits that were too decayed to be recent or of any merit to the disappearance. Tom laid the food out on the sack he had spread on the ground. The small group didn't speak, disappointed that they were no further forward than when he had left. Finally, Billoughby spoke, shattering the hot quiet air.

"I think we've exhausted our options out there. It's clear they came this way, no mistaking that. They must have gone the way of the road through the trees. That road could take a person in many directions. Time I started asking a few questions up at the Hall. Go home lads, get some rest as I may have to call on your help again soon enough." Tom gulped down his water, he had said nothing since his return. His mind was racing and try as he might he could not stop it. He would have to speak with his father alone, there was nothing else for it. But what of Elsbeth? She would surely give him up if he revealed their secret. He would sleep on it, he felt dog tired. Ed and Jimmy said their goodbyes and headed off home for a well-earned break.

"Thanks, lads, you did well." Adam jumped up into the driver's seat, his father beside him.

"You okay in the back brother? I'll drop you at the Hall father."

Tom nodded, mostly to himself.

Three

David was tired. His poor feet were bleeding and sore. They had been running for a long time now, he knew it was nighttime when the man took him from his bed.

"Keep it shut. You don't want me paying your new Ma a visit do ya!" He had hissed into the still half asleep young ears. He remembered that stench of ale from what seemed another lifetime away. He did as he was told, not wanting any harm to befall the woman that had cared for him and his sister's.

"Get a move on, you gone soft in that posh new home you 'av." David tried to keep up. He knew the voice, he heard it the night his blessed mother had passed on, he knew it from before that too. He recalled the times his mother had shut them in the cupboard while she had 'company' as she called it. He recalled also the sound of his mother's wailing as the voice took his fist to her.

"I got a pal see, he's meeting us along the Marsh road. Better not keep him waiting if ya know what's good for you runt." David tried to walk faster, the cuts were stinging and he was hot. He so wished he had finished his supper last night as he felt the rumbling pain of hunger in his stomach. Never again would he disobey Miss Mary or Miss Elsbeth. A terrible thought suddenly interrupted his thinking, what if he never got the chance to prove this. What if he never saw them or his sister's again.

"Stop ya snivellin' boy. Ain't no boy of mine a sniveller. Ya got that?" The small boy nodded, his wet face drying as quick in the heat as he forced his feet to move faster on the gravel road.

Up ahead he could see something, yes, it was a horse and cart. Maybe he could tell them he had been taken. That notion was quickly dispelled.

"Told ya, there be my old mucker as he said he would be. Right O Scrapper." The man at the helm waved his arms back in recognition.

"You get yourself up in the back, Get that cover a top o' ya mind. Don't want no busybodies getting' a look o' ya, ya hear me boy?" David nodded as he scrambled into the cart, throwing the cover over himself. It smelt like the pig pen that he was so fond of visiting, this only brought the tears gushing back to his swollen eyes once more. From under the cover, he could hear the muffled voices of the 2 men. They talked of London, then Brighton. It was clear they had no real plan between them as to where they were going. Before long David had succumbed to much-needed sleep, try as he might to stay awake.

It was dark when he awoke, dark and cold. He was no longer in the cart, that he was certain of. They must have moved him while he slept for now he was in a small room. It had the feeling of a cellar, it was cold and damp like cellars are he thought to himself as he tried to adjust his eyes.

"Decided to join us 'av ya." He did not recognise this man, this man that was shoving a plate with strange-looking slop towards him.

"You are lucky you 'av such a caring Pa, he had to go do a bit o' business see. I be lookin' out for ya see. Best eat it, ain't got no more." Pulling the plate gingerly toward him David tried to look at the man's face, it was dim in the small room and he couldn't quite see him in the shadowy light.

"Where am I?" He whispered.

"Ain't make no neva' mind where ya are boy. Ya with ya Pa and that should be enough." David had no recollection of his Pa, sure he knew various men had dealings with his mother, none that she referred to as his Pa.

The man left turning a key in the lock as he did so. The small room went black once more.

"It's going to be alright. Why I bet a whole side of ham that Miss Mary is looking for me right now." His voice was quiet in the dark and musty space. In his mind, he tried to think of all the good things that he had done since he began his new life with Miss Mary and Mrs Stanhope. There were trips to the seaside, he especially liked these for Miss Mary would buy them ice cream. They had picnics, he could almost taste the fresh bread. It was true he did not always care for the lessons, he would try harder when he was fetched back home. His mind wandered to the memory of his warm bed, when he lived with his Ma it was cold so cold that his toes would burn, the Missus house was never cold. It smelt of nice things like flowers and bread, fresh clean clothes that Sally washed then dried in the countryside air. Before bed, they would sit in their nightshirts in front of the fire listening to stories that the Missus read to them. Tales of pirates at sea, magical fairies and all manner of other wonderful things. The more David thought about his sorry situation the more he had to fight back his welling tears. If only his sister was here, not that the young fella wished her harm but he always felt that bit braver when she was around him. David drifted off to sleep, pulling the dirty rags around him as best he could.

Elsbeth ran to the door, maybe they had found him. Billoughby took off his hat as he entered, he wished he had come with better news for the red-eyed woman that stood expectantly before him, alas, he had not.
"I wonder if I could talk to those that were around on the day of young David's disappearance, I imagine they are still here as my request?" Nodding she showed the Inspector into the parlour.
"I shall send them in one at a time Inspector if that suits you?"
"It does. Please try to be positive Mrs Stanhope, we will find the lad."
"I wish I had your confidence Inspector, really I do."
Sally was the first to enter the parlour, she too had bleary eyes, the lad was sorely missed it was clear.
"Milton."
"Sally, do sit. Is there anything you can recall, any strangers hereabouts on the day?"
Sally clasped her hands on her knee as she thought. Finally, she spoke.
"Not that I can recall, the only fella I saw here was your lad. He didn't come in mind, few quiet words at the door with the Missus were all."
Billoughby was puzzled, why would one of his boys have been here? Adam certainly had no cause to come to the house, as far as Tom was concerned, surely he had been at the farm all day.

"And you are quite sure it was one of my lads?" Sally did not hesitate with her answer.

"Most definitely Sir saw your lad Tom with my own eyes. He didn't come in mind, stayed at the door talking in a hushed voice with the Mistress."

The rest of the staff were questioned with very little else to tell. Elsbeth returned to the parlour.

"Did they offer up any clues Inspector?" Billoughby shook his head, quite uncertain as to how he should tackle the visit of Tom. Hat in hand he ran his fingers around the ridge.

"Inspector?"

"Far be it from me to pry Mrs Stanhope, I have to ask you see, wouldn't seem right just because he's my flesh." Elsbeth knew what was coming. She would simply make something up, there were many reasons that Tom would have paid a call. No sense denying he was here as he was seen by Sally.

"Ah, you mean Tom. Yes, he had some business here that is true Inspector, nothing out of the ordinary."

"What might that business have been?"

"Oh, you know, something to do with our vegetable garden."

"Would he not have spoken with your gardener regarding such matters?" Elsbeth was beginning to feel uneasy.

"Yes, yes of course he would, normally. It so happens the gardener was on a break when Tom could not locate him, he came to speak with me on the matter. As I said Inspector, nothing out of the ordinary."

Billoughby had been in this profession a long time if there was an untruth being told he could spot it a mile away. There was an untruth, the question now was why.

"Thank you, Mrs Stanhope, I shall keep you updated." Leaving the Hall he knew that his next interview was going to be a most tricky one. Grace would know what to do. Strictly speaking, Billoughby knew he should not involve his wife in such matters yet he had to discuss this strange feeling with someone. Who better than his beloved.

Arriving home he could smell the familiar aroma of supper, true enough he was starved for it had been a long and weary day. Grace was in the kitchen collecting plates from the table.

"Hello, my love. We have eaten already, the boys were hungry after today's going's on." Billoughby nodded, walking over to his wife he wrapped his arms around her pulling Grace into his hold.

"Well Inspector, this is nice. I could get used to this kind of welcome." She smiled that unmistakably gentle smile kissed him gently on the cheek and pulled away to fetch supper for her weary husband.

"Sit yourself down my love." Grace knew well not to ask questions, over the years she had come to realise that should Milton wish to talk, he would talk.

"Have the boys gone out?"

"No dear, they have both retired to their beds. Cate and the little one too, daresay it will do them no harm to go up early." Billoughby supped on his tea, maybe he should not bother Grace with this after all. Chances were, that he imagined Mrs Stanhope's unwillingness to tell the truth, as he too was feeling exhausted.

Laying in bed that night he felt restless, damn this niggle he thought as he quietly pulled back the covers and headed off to the kitchen. He was surprised to see Tom sitting at the table in the flickering light of the fire.

"Can you not sleep either son?" Tom jumped in his chair as though he had been woken suddenly.

"Steady on lad, I didn't mean to put the fright into you." Touching the tea urn on the table it felt hot.

"Good lad, I was about to make a cup seems you beat me to it." Billoughby watched his son as he poured himself a mug of tea. He looked vexed sitting here in the early morning still of the house.

"I thought you would sleep longer after the day we had. Is there a thing on your mind Tom?"

"Same as all the village folks I imagine Pa, where that poor young 'en has got to."

"It is a mystery and no mistake son. Nothing happens in these parts without people knowing, yet 'tis as though he vanished into thin air." The Inspector was careful to choose his words at this point. Maybe Tom would offer something in return? Tom stared down into his mug. Would his Pa understand if he were to come clean, for a fact he knew that Sally had seen him at the Hall? Yet, what of Elsbeth, surely she would not take kindly to Tom telling all to his father. It may even cause her to end their romance, which he could not bear to do. Billoughby's heart ached for his son to come clean if only to put him out of the list of suspects. A list that presently had one solitary person on it. They sat there in silence a while longer, it seemed Tom was giving nothing away freely.

"Mrs Stanhope looked ever so beaten down this past evening, she must miss the boy terribly." Tom's eyes went up instantly at the mention of the woman, a familiar glint appearing if only for a moment. This did not go unnoticed by his father. Billoughby continued with his tact.

"Made a mention of you being over there the other day. I thought maybe she mistook the day knowing that we had spoken of this prior, you recollect you told me you had not been there?" Tom nodded.

"Did you happen to go over on that day son?" This was not good, what must he say not being privy to Elsbeth's explanation.

"I can't say for sure Pa, if I did it must have slipped my mind." Tom could not look at his Pa now, instead, he stared once again into the now cold mug that he continued to clutch in his hands.

"No matter son, we will have it straightened out soon enough. Back off to bed for me, I shouldn't wonder you do the same."

Grace slipped quietly back up the stairs, it was not her intention to eavesdrop on the pair, the conversation between the 2 gave her pause for thought. This she would discuss with her husband, it was not her way to question him on matters in front of their children but question him she must.

The morning was another bright, warm start to the day. Cate and Grace prepared breakfast as they had become accustomed to doing. Tom had left for the farm early, Billoughby not convinced his son had taken in a wink of sleep. Adam was happily cradling the baby with no particular plans for the day ahead, other than a few final touches on the cottage. It would be less than a week before they were due to move into their new home. Adam could not wait.

"You will miss us Ma when we leave." Grace smiled fondly, they had been here a while and yes, the house was small for 6 people yet she would miss them dearly.

"Not one bit, I shall stay in my nightdress all day, cook when I am hungry, wake when I want to. No, my dear, I shall not miss you." Billoughby laughed at his wife's remark.

"She will cry for a month, mark my words son."

"Of course I will miss you, all 3 of you. My only consolation is that you are not far away, I will get to see my beautiful granddaughter whenever I want to. We have indeed been a little crowded, I would not swap the time you have spent with us for anything." Cate was still grinning at her husbands face, that he would believe his mother's comment made her laugh. She knew from the moment they met that his mother adored him.

"Eat up everyone, don't let it get cold."

"Young Daisy will be here mid-morning, we have a few things to go over regarding the case if that suits you, dear?" Grace nodded toward her husband as she tucked into her breakfast plate.

"Would you like us to make ourselves scant Pa?"

"That would be a help son."

"We have a little to do at the cottage, we shall leave earlier than planned. How would my little one enjoy some sea air?" Adam cooed to the child.

"That will do her the world of good, it's been a while since we ventured to the seaside. Would you like to join us Ma?" Grace had other plans for the morning, not least a few words with her husband in private.

"That's kind of you Cate, I have errands to run. Another time perhaps."

Billoughby sat at his desk, his mind firmly fixed on the matters he could not fathom.

"Tea dear." Grace placed the mug down.

"I thought a talk now we are alone and before the young woman arrives." Billoughby pushed back his chair, he wondered what could his wife wish to discuss in private that would cause the expression she held on her face, serious where most often was content.

"Sit my love, what is bothering you?" Grace cleared her throat, why did she feel this was not going to end well?

"I followed you down here this morning, early. I have turned it over in my mind so many times and still cannot figure the better way to say it, Milton. Do you suspect our boy Tom of having something to do with young Master David's going missing?" Billoughby was shocked, not only that his wife had not made her presence known to them, that she would ask him a thing so direct. It was not her way. He stared a while at her, she held her poise. This was her son and

Grace would not bite her tongue where her children were concerned not even for her husband.

"Gracie, you must understand…"

"Milton, you must understand, our boy would never harm a hair on anyone's head least of all a child."

Milton knew this to be the case in his very core, still, the job demanded that he do things by the book or not at all, not at all was never an option in his mind.

"I cannot be seen to leave out what is convenient to me, you must see that Gracie."

"I see that if you carry on with this thought in your head it will be the undoing of us, as a family. I have rarely asked you about your work unless you have seen fit to talk a problem through but this, this is our son and he will never forgive that you could think such a thing of him. Is that what you want Milton, to push away a lad that is as close as any child can be to a parent as he is to you." Billoughby shook his head. It was unfortunate, it had to be looked into and that was the nature of the job. The knock at the front door cut through the silent atmosphere.

"That will be Daisy. We can talk more about this later." Grace turned to let the guest in, she paused.

"If your answer is the same there is little need for further discussion." She left Billoughby to way up the consequences of his words.

"Hello dear, do come in. The Inspector is in the study, go through." Daisy sensed that things in the usually happy household were not as they should be.

David had been given a bowl of what looked like pig food for his breakfast, he struggled in his attempt to eat it. Even at their worst times with his departed mother, he had never been asked to eat anything of this like. He had not slept well, the room was dark and even with the warm weather of the past months, it felt as cold as ice during the night hours. His face was red with the tears he had shed in the fitful dark wakings that had come to him often.

"Hurry up with that, we got work to do." Bellowed the man that had been left in charge of him. What that work was, David had no idea. He pushed the bowl back across the floor to the impatient fella that stood guard.

"Suit ya self. Won't be any more offerings this day I tell ya' boy."
David decided he would rather go hungry than eat the swill he was
given. Grabbing him by the collar the man thrust him out into the
corridor.

"' Er, get these on." He handed the child a pair of dirty shorts which
the boy hastily pulled on, if nothing else they would keep his legs
warmer.

"Where are we going?" he asked quietly.

"Like I say we got work to do." The morning air was a relief for the
child, he breathed it in slowly, thankful he was out of the squalid
room. The man tugged the child along for some way. David tried to
figure out where they were but in truth he had no idea. He knew it
was not Canterbury, and he knew it was not his quiet little village.
The streets were filled with grand houses unlike any he had seen
before. As they rounded the corner the child's eyes grew as large as
the moon, the sight before him was one of splendour. Did they mean
to put him to work in this place? It had the look of a faraway castle
in a book that the missus had read to them, Ali something, thought
the boy. Lost in his thoughts he did not notice the man coming
toward them until the strangely familiar voice began to speak.

"Didn't give ya any trouble did he?"

"Nah Archie, little 'en like 'im give me trouble. I'd box his ears I
would." The man did not loosen his grip on David's collar as the
men continued on the street talking of the plan they had for the
coming day.

"Boy, see that place?" He pointed to the imposing building,
wagging his dirty fingers in mid-air.

"That's where the toffs go, see. Ya know how to run boy?" David
nodded, if there was one thing he could do well it was to run.

"My friend 'ere has a coin in his coat pocket, I want you to put your
hand in there quiet like and take it."

"That's stealing. Miss Mary said it's not right to steal a person's
things." Archie raised his hand into the air.

"Hang on fella, the lad will do as ya said, ain't need for a walloping.
Ya not lookin' for a wallop are you boy?" David shook his head as
he stared up at the man's fist.

"Now, do what he said, take the coin." The small boy reached into
the deep pocket, his tiny fingers searching out the item. He fished it
out presenting it to the man Archie.

"That's better. We get in there through the side door, see, Scrapper will be out here so no getting it in ya head to run off, and mind my words boy if you do I might 'av to pay that new ma of yours a visit" David understood the man all too well as he trudged into the gardens of the large building.

Once inside the tradesmen's entrance, the man wasted no time setting him to work. David would walk amongst the crowds, dipping his hands into various pockets then placing them in the man's bag. This continued for most of the day until a porter spotted them and asked the pair to leave.

Outside Scrapper was waiting.

"How d'ya get on?"

"Well enough before someone got sloppy." He glared at David now as though to make his point to the young boy. The day did not end there. The man and Scrapper found their way to a local ale inn, no doubt to drink their expected profits of the day down the drain. David was instructed to sit quietly.

"If ya know what's good for ya." The youngster did as he was bid, sitting in silence as the men drank themselves into a stupor. It was dark when the woman from the bar approached him.

"Isn't it time you were in bed young man?" she asked.

"Don't know Missus, I ain't been in a place like this." She smiled a warm, friendly smile.

"This your Pa?" David shook his head.

"I don't think so, missus." She looked puzzled. Why would a youngster be with people that he didn't seem to know?

"You alright luvvy?"

"I would rather be at home." After a quick look around she beckoned the boy to stand, David quietly followed her to the bar.

"Why don't you get yourself off home luvvy. You know the way?" David nodded, in truth, he had no idea where he was but, was glad of the permission given by the woman. Opening the door she slipped a bun into his hand.

"Something for on the way." She smiled as she quietly pushed the door closed behind him.

David stood in the road for a moment, it was dark. He thought it best to get under cover somewhere before the pair were roused as they surely would be when the inn closed for the night. The boy began to walk, this turned into a steady run, the further away he got the better.

"What d'ya mean you ain't seen a nipper, he was sat right there." Shouted the man.

"I am sorry Sir, It's been a busy night and I don't have time to keep a watch on everyone that walks through that door." Scrapper scratched his chin, he peered around the now empty inn.

"He ain't 'ere." The other man was furious now, he pushed the door open with a force that nearly took it off its hinge.

"When I find that scag of a boy I will take my fist to his face you see if I don't."

Scrapper walked quickly trying to keep up with his angry partner. Wouldn't like to be in the lad's place when he finds him, thought the large drunken man.

By the time they had gotten back to their rooms, the boy was long gone. He ran until he could run no more, not daring to stop to eat the bun for fear of being caught. Spotting the boat on the shore he climbed over the side, making himself comfortable under a pile of thick nets only then did he dare to take a bite of the much-needed item of food.

David slept, as he did he dreamt. He was riding on the back of Miss Mary's horse with the motion of a comforting one as his body was rocked gently. The sky was blue as they galloped through lush green meadows that backed Robert's farmland.

"STOP!" The booming voice awoke him from his slumber. A hand reached under the nets, pulling him out by his shoulder.

"Lookin' like we have a stowaway, Freddie. What you doing on 'ere lad?" Looking around him David could see water, lots and lots of water. He wondered if they were on their way to another place. Was he ever going to get home? His tears came thick and fast, try as he might he could not stop the panicked feeling that rose in his chest.

"Calm yourself, lad, you're in no danger here. Can't speak for your ma when she finds you gone."

"Ain't got no ma Sir, no pa neither." The man they called Freddie stared at the boy then shaking his head went into the cabin. He returned a few moments later with a mug and a plate.

"Hungry lad?" David nodded, he was starved. He took the mug of tea and plate gratefully. The men spoke quietly as he ate, he paid no real attention to what they said, he was far too busy concentrating on the hot food and how much he could get in his mouth before he woke again.

"Slow down lad, you'll choke." The youngster smiled up at the fisherman as he continued to eat.

"It's not your day today lad, we're bound for Rye so if you were thinking of getting back to Brighton this day I'm afraid it isn't happening." David knew that name. Miss Elsbeth had talked about the place many a time. That meant it must be close to home, mustn't it?

"You strong lad?" David nodded for he thought himself strong for his age.

"Good, no freeloaders aboard this here trawler. Make yourself busy, lets see if you can't get those nets stretched out for me to have a look at." The boy jumped up and began pulling the heavy nets this way and that until he had them spread neatly across the deck.

"' Ey not too bad youngster. Right, let's have a look at them." The fisherman inspected the nets carefully, stopping every so often to stroke his chin or scratch his head.

"You did a grand job of it lad. How are you at washing dishes?" He pointed to the cabin.

"I can do that Sir."

"Off with you then lad, the bucket is on the floor, dishes on the top." David busied himself dipping the plates and mugs into the cold water, stopping only to eat what was left on them for he wasn't sure when his next meal would be. Freddie watched him from the deck. What kind of life must this little fella have had he wondered.

"Going soft there Freddie?"

"Beggars belief that there's youngster's that age fending for themselves is all." He called over to David.

"Make sure you get them lot clean as you can lad, don't want the crew getting sick do we?" David nodded, holding a clean plate up to show.

"Good man, keep at it." Freddie found many different tasks for David that kept the young boy occupied for the rest of the day, David did not complain once.

Four

Billoughby waved his wife goodbye as he set off for the station. The search had gone as far as it could, the Inspector had leads to follow up in Canterbury. Billoughby had no intention of leaving out any possible connections to the young boy that may have been overlooked. Starting in Canterbury seemed as good a place as any to start as the area the boy had been born. Reverend Moore had been a great help in collating all the information he could from the time he first retrieved the children from the squalor they had been residing in. A notebook with names had been amongst the belongings which the Reverend had thought important to throw into the small case. Daisy had made light work the previous day of deciphering the scrawl into a legible list.

"However did you manage it so quickly." He had asked the woman.

"Quite easy when you have a father that writes the way mine does." She laughed.

"Still, I would never have made sense of it, you're a credit to this job." Daisy was quietly pleased with the acknowledgement of her skills, it wasn't often she was praised in her previous post.

On arrival at the station, Billoughby was pleased to spot his old friend Joseph, he waved across the road.

"Well fancy meeting you here today, are you arriving or, leaving?" Joseph grinned.

"Arriving dear friend, I have a meeting in Canterbury, and you?"

"I too have a few calls to make in Canterbury, I would be glad of the company." The 2 men walked to the platform catching up on home matters as they did so.

"Any news of the boy Milton. It is a dreadful thing to have a child of that age simply vanish."

"Not as yet, I'm hoping I can gain some information on this trip. There must be somebody out there that knows something of his whereabouts."

"You think the boy still lives?" Billoughby stopped walking, his face grew serious. It had not entered his mind that David could have fallen prey to such finality.

"I never gave that a thought if I'm truthful Joseph. You don't think that do you?" Joseph looked at his friend, he hadn't intended to upset the man and yet, it was something they may be forced to accept.

"I think, dear chap, that you should not rule it out." The journey to Canterbury was a quieter one than first anticipated. Billoughby lost in the what if's, Joseph kicking himself for bringing the matter to the forefront of his friend's mind. They arrived at the station and bid each other farewell.

"Maybe see you on the way back, good luck dear chap."

The first port of call for the Inspector was to be the police headquarters, if he could run a check on some of the names on the list it might give him an insight into their current abodes, not to mention any criminal records that may be useful to know beforehand. He stopped to make small talk with the few officers he knew as he made his way through the building.

"Inspector Billoughby, I wasn't expecting to see you here. Can we help you in some way?" The Inspector nodded towards the secretary, she had been working at the HQ a long time.

"Good morning Patty, I have a list of names that I will need to see records you hold if any."

"You are fortunate we have a quiet morning, give that to me and have a seat, may take some time it is quite a list."

"Yes, sorry about that. It is appreciated." Patty went into the back office to find the information needed. 10 minutes had passed when the woman returned.

"Go fetch yourself a drink Inspector, this is going to be a while."

"Maybe I will stretch my legs, see you in half an hour." The woman waved over her shoulder as she left the room.

Making his way down the cobbled street the Inspector stopped a while. He stared up at the house he had once had cause to deal with. The house formally owned by Stanhope lay empty now, as Mrs Stanhope had no desire to take it on, or for that matter have any dealings with it, it would seem. He carried on, it felt a long time since that business and yet, it had barely been a year ago if that. It was a pleasant walk, Canterbury in the sunshine always had a good feel about it. The grand cathedral stood out way above the other packed in buildings, its tall towers magnificently set against the backdrop of the blue sky. It was busy of course, it was always busy here, with people bustling to and fro from houses and businesses alike. Billoughby smiled, he liked the place mostly, yet he could never imagine living in such a seemingly crowded, cramped area. No, he would not give up the country life for all the money in the world.

"Inspector. Enjoy your walk?"
"I did thank you. Did you find anything for me?" The woman handed him a piece of paper.
"Quite a group of friends this woman had, mostly low-level thieving, drunken behaviour, that sort of thing. One of interest I put a line under. See, just here." Billoughby glanced at the list, it was more than he had expected.
"You are a diamond Patty, thank you so much." The addresses were a start, he was well aware that they may have changed over time, or that they may never have been legitimate in the first place. Still, all leads had to be followed if they were to have a chance at finding David.
The name underlined was that of a Mr Archie Spires.
"Why is this name important Patty?"
"It turns out that this fella was usually the one that came to collect the deceased woman whenever she got pulled for loitering, they shared an address for a time, goes back a good few years too." Billoughby thanked the woman again and left. He would have to make quick work of this if he were to catch the train back at a reasonable hour.
The first address he went to wasn't that far from the station. It looked bleak from the outside even in this glorious sunshine.
Tapping on the door he did not expect to get a response, wrong, the door opened slowly revealing a young girl of around 5. She had dirty

matted hair and wore an oversized shirt that looked like it had never seen the inside of a washtub.

"Hello miss. Is your Mother or Father home?" The small child stepped back, pulling the door wider as she did so. Not sure if this was an invitation Billoughby stood his ground on the cobbled path.

"Who is it?" Came the call from inside.

"My name is Billoughby, I'm looking for Mr Burrows." The child disappeared down the dark hallway.

"Get yourself in here then." Came the reply. Billoughby stepped in, not something he would have recommended to junior officers, especially as he was alone.

"In here." Called the man.

"Mr Burrows?"

"That's me, how can I help you?" The room was dingy, as were many in the area. The smell was that of old ale and something unpleasant that he couldn't quite recognise.

"My name is Billoughby, I believe you were, or are an acquaintance of Mr Spires?"

The man jumped from his seat, he was a large fella when he stood.

"I know of him, it's true. Wouldn't say we were ever pals or the like. What has the beggar done now?"

"You know of his whereabouts?" The man scratched his head as he pondered the question.

"Heard he was heading for Brighton, good riddance if you ask me. Get's up to no good that one. Does he owe you?"

"Not exactly. I'm a police Inspector." The man's expression changed from that of relaxed to worried.

"Listen, I don't want any trouble. Whatever he's done is nothing to do with me."

Billoughby smiled, more to put the large fella at ease.

"I don't want any trouble either friend, all I am interested in is his whereabouts or likely places he might stay in Brighton. There will be no mention of our meeting here today if that's what bothers you. He has taken something, so we believe and we would very much like that something back."

"He had a woman that he knocked around with, she's dead now lord love her. He had her into all sorts if you get my meaning." The Inspector nodded as the man continued to talk.

"Few kiddies she had, God himself knows what happened to them, workhouse I shouldn't wonder. Archie, well he and Scrapper had some scheme, very cagey about it they were. Archie said it would be his big break, last time he was at the Inn he had a skinful, telling all and sundry that he was off to make his fortune in Brighton. There's a place he used to go, Obed Arms if I'm not mistaken. You could try there I suppose, if he's in Brighton I'd put money on him giving that place a visit. Word of warning, he's a wrong 'en, fights dirty too." Billoughby was busy scribbling in his notepad when he stopped.

"What do you mean, he fights dirty?" The man puffed hard on his cigarette.

"He almost always has a knife of sorts on him, not bothered about using it neither."

"Thanks for the warning. Do you know where this inn is situated? Not being too familiar with the area, it would be a help."

"Dinapore Street as I recall, not far from the seafront." Billoughby tucked his pad into his pocket.

"You have been a great help, I will keep your name out of it." Placing his hand into his jacket he pulled out some coins.

"Treat the little one to something, thank you." The man took the coins, he didn't hesitate which the Inspector was glad about.

"Good luck, I hope you can get back whatever it is you lost."

There did not seem any real reason for the Inspector to trawl the streets of Canterbury, he had more than enough to be going on with from Mr Burrows. It was a fine start and he was pleased the man had been so informative. Standing on the platform he heard the familiar sound of his friend behind him.

"Hello, dear chap, twice in one day. Did you get what you needed?"

"Hello Joseph, I did thank you, more than I expected too. How was your day?"

"Oh, you know, same as ever." The 2 men boarded the train for Ashford, both happy in their accomplishments of the day. The chatter was light on the return journey with Joseph regaling stories of home life, Billoughby talking of Adam and Cate's new home with their imminent moving.

"I imagine it will be nice to get the space back after all this time?" Billoughby laughed.

"Truth is, we have loved having them especially the little one. Watching her grow and get her own little ways, that cottage was not built for 6, times a man needs a bit of breathing room, Joseph, few and far between they have been." Joseph nodded in agreement.

" I can understand that, and we have a big house, still a person needs thinking space am I right?" Billoughby tossed an idea around his mind, Joseph watched him carefully.

"Out with it." The Inspector laughed again, his friend knew him well.

"It's Tom, I worry about that lad. You know we have this missing boy, I asked Tom had he been to the house, no, he tells me. Turns out he had. Why do you think he would keep that from me, Joseph?" Joseph shrugged, it was a predicament he did not envy the Inspector.

"Maybe it slipped his mind. Have you asked him about it?" Billoughby shook his head.

"Not in an official way, but that will have to come. Gracie is angry at the mere idea of it, yet what can I do?" Joseph felt for his friend, but that was the way it had to be done and they both knew it.

"Could he have a reason to be there, personal I mean?"

"Not that he's telling me. There are a couple of local girls that work over there, maybe he's stuck on one of them, too embarrassed to let on?" Joseph sighed, he had no real help to give his friend other than to do what he had to.

"Either way, it has to be looked into. I shall tackle it before I head to Brighton." Joseph had a thought.

"Why not take the lad with you, might help for you to have some time together and that way you can work your questions in along the way." This was a good idea, the Inspector would give it some consideration.

"This is why you have the big house, my clever friend."

Tom sat in the field waiting, not sure if Elsbeth would turn up given the situation with David. The sun shone down bathing the now golden grass in a glorious haze, in the distance, Tom spotted a figure. Raising his hands to shield the bright rays he tried to focus. Was it her? He stood to get a better view.

"Tom, is that you?" The voice although familiar was not that of his Elsbeth, instead, it was the voice of the Thompson girl. She quickened her step, soon she was standing in front of the young man.

"I thought it was you. What are you doing out here alone?" Tom shrugged, disappointed that it wasn't Elsbeth.

"Hello, nothing much. How are you, Miss Thompson?" The young woman looked annoyed.

"Would you please call me Esther?" She almost snapped back at him.

"How is the family?"

"They are well thank you, Master Billoughby." 2 can play this game she thought. Tom could not help but smile at the response.

"That's good to hear. Are you going anywhere or, just out for a walk?"

"I was on my way up to the Hall, I believe the Mistress there is looking for a kitchen help, beats sitting at home with the little ones." Tom nodded, although he could not help but wonder if this would put him in an even trickier situation. Behind the Thompson girl he saw a figure, the person stood and watched the pair, turned and disappeared through the trees. Great, this was all he needed, this girl was beginning to cause him more trouble every time he was in contact with her.

"I shan't keep you." He called as he began to walk away, his pace brisk.

"Wait, Tom, wait." But he was already gone. Esther stood alone in the field shaking her head. What was wrong with this fella?

Tom ran as fast as his legs would carry him through the trees, almost falling over the shrubs that entwined in the dampness of the undergrowth, he could see Elsbeth ahead of him.

"Are you going to make me run?" he called out. No answer came as she continued on her way. Maybe she didn't hear me, he consoled his mind. He was within touching distance when they reached the lane, right at the very moment Mr Nash came by on his cart.

"Can I offer you a ride?" He asked the woman.

"That would be ever so good of you, it is tiring in this heat." She turned to face Tom.

"Oh, hello there Mr Billoughby, I did not see you there. Give my regards to your parents won't you." Climbing up on the cart she looked at the young man, her eyes red and tear-stained.

"I will do that. Any news of young David?" Shaking her head her face turned from his as Mr Nash pulled away.

"Bye young Tom." He was gone, as was his Elsbeth.

Tom walked slowly back to the farm, he had finished his work for the day yet, he did not want to go home just yet.

"Can't keep away eh?" Laughed Robert as the young man slumped into the chair. Tom remained quiet. Robert had noticed his melancholy mood for some time now.

"Do you want to talk about it son?" How could he? How could he talk to anyone about this? Tom wished he could, this was a small community that did not take kindly to a relationship such as his.

"I best not, thank you, Robert." The older man scratched his head, he knew that look. He knew it because it was the one he had worn for so long until his Mary had come back into his life.

"Listen, son, I am neither gossip nor one that judges other people. I pride myself on these things. If you have something you need to get off your chest, I am here and, it'll go no further. Not even to the Mrs." Tom did not doubt this for a second, what he didn't want was the man telling him what the 'right thing' to do would be.

"It's a very private problem, Robert, I am grateful for the offering, don't think I'm not. Trouble is, I can't tell you." Robert shrugged, he had given it his best shot and if the lad didn't want to talk.

"It's never as bad as it seems, that's all I'll say. Come on lad, let's go over to the Inn, don't know about you but I could do with something to ease my thirst." The 2 men set off for a well-earned mug of ale.

Elsbeth arrived back at the hall in time to greet Esther.

"Come in Miss Thompson, I shall be with you in a moment." She led the girl into the kitchen, hanging her hat in the closet she stopped to wipe her face. The tears and dust had left it gritty, this would not do she thought.

"Now, I understand you are seeking a position in the house, the kitchen wasn't it?" Esther nodded.

"Yes, Mrs Stanhope. Sally had mentioned it to my Ma, said I should call by and ask you about it." Elsbeth sat down across the large wooden table from the girl. My, but she was a pretty thing, full of a youthfulness that Elsbeth could barely remember. It seemed so long ago that she had looked as fresh-faced as the youngster before her now. It wasn't at all surprising that Tom would find her pleasing to look upon, her own features now showing the signs of many lives lived, heartaches that she had lost count of.

"Mrs Stanhope?" Esther brought her back from the thoughts that spun in her head.

"Yes, I take it you can cook, and do household chores satisfactorily?"

"I can Mrs Stanhope, Ma tells me my cooking gets better every day, cleaning chores, I do most of them at home as Ma has her hands full with the little ones." Elsbeth nodded.

"Your Ma won't miss the help you give her?"

"No Mrs Stanhope, our Bessie is taking over from me so Ma will still have some help."

"You have a young man so I hear?" Elsbeth knew this was not an appropriate question, she could not help herself." The young girl smiled, her face flushed with colour.

"We are working on it Mrs Stanhope, he will come around Pa reckons, bit shy is all."

"You have plans to wed?"

"Aye, one day. He doesn't know it yet, needs a kick up the pants but we'll get there." Elsbeth had to bite down hard on her lip to curb her reaction, so that's what they were doing in their field today, making plans.

"I am sure he does, rightly so. You will live in for the position, is that a problem?" Esther was taken aback at this, neither Sally nor her Ma had spoken of her having to live at the old creepy house. She gulped, can't turn it down over one silly thing.

"That's not a problem for me Mrs Stanhope."

"It seems simpler to do this, the children wake quite early. It makes sense to have someone here to get the fires started before they awaken. Winter will soon be upon us." Esther nodded, put that way it did make sense. It could get fiercely bitter in the winter.

"Good, that's settled. Shall I expect you on Monday? That will give you the weekend to sort out anything that needs to be moved here, your clothes and such like." The chair scraped on the polished floor as the Lady of the house stood, she looked at the young woman again then left the room.

Standing at the doorway Sally smiled.

"All went as it should?"

"I start Monday, I'm to live in," replied Esther.

"We best sort a room for you then, come with me. It will be at the top of the house, just yourself. None of the staff lives in, happen the Missus knows what she's doing." Esther followed the cheery woman up several flights of stairs. The rooms were almost attic spaces, they had once been occupied by the staff in Mary's younger days at the hall. Some were bigger than others, all had cots if a little dusty.

"Make yourself useful and fetch up a bucket of warm soapy water to give this one a wipe down, I'll open the window to air the place, 'tis stuffy in here and no mistake." Sally rattled on oblivious to Esther having left the room. The girl returned with a bucket filled with suddy water and rags.

"Terrible hot up here."

"Be terrible cold in the winter too, you mark my words and be sure to bring some thick nightshirts with you."

Downstairs Elsbeth was sitting staring through the window in the study. What had possessed her to have the girl live in? It wasn't as though she lived miles away! She lived in the village, not a 15-minute walk away. Shaking her head she began writing her weekly correspondence. She heard the clatter of horses hooves outside, she did not look up. It was more than likely a grocery delivery having placed one with Mr Nash earlier in the week.

"Inspector here to see you, Mrs Stanhope." The very words filled her with an equal amount of anticipation and dread.

"Show him in please Sally."

"Good afternoon, Mrs Stanhope. I hope I'm not disturbing you?"

"Not at all Inspector. Do you have news?" Billoughby did not have the kind of news the worried face was hoping for. He sat, he wasn't asked to yet he felt weary after his day of travel.

"I have no definite news I'm sorry to say, Mrs Stanhope. However, I have got some addresses of a man that claims to be the boys' father, or so I'm led to believe. I have spoken to a chap that knows the places this man frequents in Brighton." Elsbeth ran her hands across her hair, this was all going far too slowly for her.

"Then why are you here and not in Brighton, if you have information surely there is no time to be paying house calls that are taking up valuable time." Billoughby knew the woman was filled with worry, he knew if it had been one of his own he would be asking the same question.

"I will be leaving for Brighton tomorrow, I thought it courteous to keep you as informed as is possible Mrs Stanhope." Elsbeth stood, what a frightful person all of this turmoil was turning her into.

"Excuse me, Inspector, I have barely slept for the worry of it all. Tea, you must be parched." Billoughby nodded, he would be grateful for a cup.

"I intend to take my boy Tom along with me." He peered closely at her, trying to glimpse a reaction at his son's name. There it was.

"Do you recall the day before David disappeared Mrs Stanhope? Tom came here did he not?" Elsbeth felt uncomfortable with this line of quizzing.

"A great many of the locals call here for one reason or another, Inspector. Did Tom say he was here?"

"Tea would be just the thing, thank you. Simply a question Mrs Stanhope." She did not respond with the story of the gardener, maybe, just maybe it had been something and nothing. Elsbeth rang the bell for tea, the pair sitting quietly until Sally arrived with the tray.

"The other children, how are they?" He asked.

"They are well thank you, Doris asks questions, of course, I have no answer for the poor mite. What am I supposed to tell her?" What indeed, it must be difficult for the woman.

"They are here today?" continued Billoughby as he sipped his tea.

"Mary has taken them to the seaside, bless her, I don't know what I would do without her in all of this."

"She is so very different to how I first remember her, our meeting back last year. Marriage suits her. Is it something you, yourself are considering again, once we have this unfortunate incident solved?" Elsbeth looked startled. Is that the kind of thing she was expected to contemplate at a time like this?

"Forgive me, Mrs Stanhope. I don't know what I was thinking, silly question. Good tea." The Inspector was struggling to make small talk. He had no more information regarding the boy that he had not already shared. Sensing the awkward mood in the air, Elsbeth offered a weak smile.

"Maybe one day Inspector. Who knows what the Almighty has in store for any of us."

"Speaking of which, Reverend Moore asked me to pass on his prayers, he may call on you tomorrow, vague with the timing as he ever is." Nodding her agreement of the Reverend's disorganised way of things she placed her cup back on the saucer.

"If you have no further need of me Inspector, I must get on." Billoughby rose to his feet, placing his hat back atop his head he made for the door.

"If you do remember anything, no matter how unimportant you may think it, please let me know. It all helps one way or the other. I'll see myself out. Good day Mrs Stanhope, please try to get some rest if you can."

David liked the boat, he could get used to this life, he was fed, kept warm and the fella's aboard were so much nicer than he had first thought. Not at all like the pirate's Miss Mary had warned them about in her stories. Yes, if he could no longer go back to the Missus at the hall this life would do very nicely, very nicely indeed!

"All done in there nipper?" It was Freddie that broke the thoughts of the child.

"Aye, aye Captain." Smiled the child as he placed the remaining dry dishes in the box. Freddie had told him that should the sea be rough, as is often the case, this would stop them flying all over the cabin.

"What are you going to do when we get to Rye young David?" David shrugged, he knew it was a place often talked about in the village, how far it was he could not be sure.

"We've been talking, the fella's and me, be no trouble for you to stay awhile with us. Turns out you're a better sailor than I imagined you'd be. Not had such clean dishes for a long time too! Ferret's good an' all but he don't clean them as good as you do." David laughed, Ferret was a very old sailor that if he wasn't whistling, he was singing, whatever else he did aboard, David wasn't entirely sure.

"Think about it lad, we're in no hurry to throw you overboard." Curled up in his makeshift cot, David drifted off to sleep. He felt better than he had since the time that they had taken him.

The trawler bobbed gently on the water, the fishermen, happy to take their time with the journey sat on the deck swilling down grog, one of the sidelines that topped up their wage. One by one they dispersed to their own areas for much-needed sleep. Freddie took first watch, as was often his way. He stared up at the starry night sky, he thought about his lost family. The excitement of a long-awaited child that had turned to unbelievable sorrow when his beloved wife and son were taken from him. He would often look at the stars, imagining that they were up there somewhere keeping a watchful eye on him.

"Silly ole' sod." He said aloud.

"Who you talking to?" Whispered a bleary-eyed David. Freddie turned to the youngster.

"' Him up there young fella. What you doing awake anyhow?"

David stared up at the sky, he could not see 'Him, whoever that was.

"I needed to go."

"Feel better?" David nodded as he sidled up to the man. Freddie, ruffling the youngster's hair, patted his knee. The child clambered up to sit and stare with the man that had shown him such kindness.

"See the face on the moon?"

"Yes, Miss Mary said many folks think the moon is cheese, is that true?" Freddie laughed, he made no mention of Miss Mary or, who she might be. That would come in its own time.

"Reckon if it was cheese, the Lord Almighty himself would have had it away on a nice bit of crusty bread, eh?" It was an hour or so before Freddie gently placed the sleeping child carefully back in his makeshift bed.

Five

Daisy knocked quietly at the door, it was still early and she wasn't sure if Mrs Billoughby was awake. The door opened slowly.

"Good morning Tom, is the Inspector still here." Tom was dressed, biting down on a piece of fresh bread.

"He should be, I'm to accompany Pa so, if he's left already, he's done so without me. Come in, I'll give him a shout."

Daisy made her way into the kitchen, Grace was busy clearing the breakfast things away.

"There was I trying not to waken the house, the house is all up and running." She smiled at the woman.

"Time for a cup?" Grace motioned for the young policewoman to sit.

"That would be lovely Mrs Billoughby. I only stopped by to give the Inspector this map, of where to find the place he's going to. Oh, and to beg a day off for I'm to have a visitor from London." The beaming smile on her face said more than the short afterthought of a sentence.

"Sounds very exciting, do we know of the young man in question?" Daisy's face flushed crimson.

"Why Mrs Billoughby, I don't recall saying it was a gentleman." Grace dried her hands on the teatowel.

"No, but your face did."

"It's the chap we met while we were there on *that* case."

"Ah, I see. Have you been corresponding with him?" Daisy could not contain her delight, she was bursting to tell somebody.

"We have, oh, Mrs Billoughby he is so, so nice. Not like some, real gent he is. He wants to come to visit as he has something to ask me, I am that excited. Nervous too, yes, very nervous. I mean, he could wish to ask me about cows or the countryside or, any of the other things that are not at all about marriage."

"What's this about marriage?" Billoughby asked, straightening his tie as he entered the room.

"Good morning Sir, here are the details you asked for. Reverend Moore sure does know a lot about a lot of things, he said to go easy when you get into the place, they're not always happy to see people of our profession in there." Billoughby scanned the drawing, its directions marked out meticulously.

"Excellent. Now, what did I hear about marriage? Planning on leaving us so soon Daisy?"

"No Sir, just that, well, I wonder if I could take the day off tomorrow to have a visitor. I know we are in the middle of this search, I understand it comes first." Billoughby tucked the map into his jacket pocket.

"You've earned a day off my girl, enjoy it. I hear it's set to rain at last come the weekend."

"Ready Pa?" Tom was waiting by the door, he could not wait to get away for a few hours even if it meant going to a place he didn't know.

"Ready son, you have the lunch, my love?" Grace passed the basket of food to Tom.

"Try to be back for tomorrow. It would be nice to have a meal, all of us together before Cate and Adam move into the cottage. Daisy, you are welcome to bring your visitor."

"I may hold you to that Mrs Billoughby, I still cannot match you in the kitchen, don't want to scare him off do I?"

The train journey would be a long one, Billoughby had set his mind on an early start hoping to take full advantage of the hours that they would spend in Brighton.

"If the lad isn't there I see no point in wasting precious time in the area." Tom had agreed, they had no real reasons to think they would find David in Brighton, a hope yes, but nothing solid.

Billoughby wondered if he should broach the subject of his son's visit to the hall once again, it was troubling him for so many reason's, not least the fact that should the locals discover he had not questioned his son it would cause more trouble than he needed. It was a small village, close-knit and any opportunity to cast aspersions would be grasped with both hands. He thought about Grace, she had been furious when he raised the subject. Under normal circumstances, he would have agreed with her, this was far from normal a child had gone missing. Tom was busy watching out of the window, his thoughts firmly on Elsbeth. What had upset her yesterday, surely it wasn't as simple as seeing him talking with the Thompson girl? He could not understand the fairer sex that was true. His mind wandered to the day before the boy's disappearance, it had been a blissful afternoon.

"That's a smile you have on your face there, son. Want to share?" Tom sat up straight, he had not realised he was smiling, he felt foolish as he quickly straightened himself.

"Nothing interesting, Pa."

"Not what it looked like son. You know Tom, I've been meaning to talk to you about something." Billoughby paused, as he tried to phrase the words in his head.

"Yes, father?" Billoughby lowered his voice as he leant closer to Tom.

"It's about this visit of yours to the hall. Now, I don't want you to get upset again but you must understand that I have a duty to question all that were over there on that day. If you have a secret that you would rather not share, I get it, trouble is son, it won't look good for you if folks find out. Do you understand what I'm saying, Tom?" Tom could feel the hair on the back of his neck prickle, he knew in his heart that his father was simply doing his job, yet he had no answer, not one he could give at any rate.

"I told you, father, I don't see why we have to keep on going over this." His voice was low, an angry hiss that told Billoughby to back off.

"We have to keep going over it, son, because that's what I do." Tom shook his head, a defiant wall had gone up.

"You know I can't leave it?"

"I don't suggest you do, father, you have your job and I, have my reasons. All I will say is that I had nothing to do with the boy's disappearance, you can choose to believe me, your son, or you can continue down this road."

"You are not making this easy son."

"I have nothing more to say on the matter, father." Billoughby sat back, too bloody like his father this one in that he never gave anything away. A good quality for a member of the force thought Billoughby but not what you need from a family member. The remainder of the long journey was mostly in silence making it feel an awkward one. They ate a small portion of the neatly packed goodies that Grace had prepared.

Daisy fussed around the rectory, plumping cushions and flicking the odd particles of dust from the wooden furniture as she waited for her guest.

"Heavens girl you will take the shine off that cabinet if you dust it one more time." Complained Tobias Moore, his face smiling at the nervousness of the young woman.

"I doubt I have seen the place looking so polished since Mary first took it on. Your guest will have no interest in how dust-free the place is, I am sure he means to visit you and not observe the state of our home. Sit down and drink your tea." Daisy reluctantly sat.

"So sorry Reverend, I am that twisted up inside, I want everything to be perfect."

"And you say you have no idea what the chap wants?"

"No, Julian, that is Mr Richardson is very coy in his letter. He says only that he has a question for me, no more, no less. What if he proposes Reverend, what must I do?" Tobias grinned, he was so fond of this woman in the way a man would be of a daughter.

"Then I shall put him through some rigorous interrogation, see if I don't. We cannot have just anybody whisking you off now can we?" Daisy wasn't sure she liked the sound of this, her expression turning into a frown.

"I would not dear girl, you really ought not to worry until you know what it is he has to say."

Easy for you to say, she thought.

"Will you stay in the rectory with us Reverend?" Tobias patted her hand.

"Is that what you would like, I am happy to make myself busy in the church if it suits you better?" Daisy did not know what she was to do, was it proper for her to accept a visit without a chaperone?

"For the time being I would rather you stayed, is that acceptable Reverend?"

"Of course, my dear. Whatever makes you comfortable."

They did not have to wait too long, the bell rang at the precise moment the clock chimed 12.

"I'm not ready, I'm not ready for this." Daisy went into a panic at the sound of the bell being pulled.

"Compose yourself, my dear, I shall let the man in." Before Daisy had time to protest, Tobias could be heard in the hall.

"Hello, please come in. I am Reverend Moore, you may call me Tobias. Please follow me through to the parlour. Daisy, Daisy dear, your guest has arrived."

Daisy was already standing, the nervous look disappearing the minute Julian came into view.

"My dear Miss Billoughby, or should that be Miss Harvey? It has been too long." Julian dispensed with etiquette as, to the surprise of Tobias, he swept the speechless woman almost off her feet in a warm, all-embracing hug.

"How are you today lad? Did you sleep well?" David could see by the position of the sun that he had slept, not only well but, quite late into the morning. Rubbing his eyes in the glare of the bright rays he nodded.

"Did I miss breakfast?" He was hungry. Looking around he could see they were approaching land.

"I left some in the cabin for you lad, ship-shape now, we'll be docking soon enough." The men on board were busy preparing their catch, sorting into this crate and that. Some of the crates contained bottles that were swiftly covered up with straw then layered with fish across the top before the lids were firmly placed. The trawler made its way into Rye harbour. It was a busy little area this morning, with various crafts of smaller variety unloading crates and suchlike. The buzz in the air filled David with excitement, he had not seen anything like it in his young life.

"Make yourself useful nipper, grab my pouch and come with me."

"Aye Captain." Called the overwhelmed boy as he snatched the pouch and ran to follow Freddie off the boat. Freddie made his way over to a stout man that was arguing with another fella.

"Deals a deal matey, take it or leave it." The disgruntled man snatched a bag of coin, muttering curses under his breath.

"Now you stick close by me son, you hear?" David nodded at the instruction.

"Took your time Freddie, who be this now?" He added as he pointed at the small child hiding behind Freddie's coattails. Freddie gently eased David forward.

"My sister's boy thought I'd show him the world. Right, down to business. I got what you ordered, no funny business mind, it's in the crates marked with a cross, the rest is the catch. Have a look, see what you have a mind to settle on." The man, made his way over to the crates that had been unloaded, lifting lids he sifted quickly through the cargo.

"That'll do, the rest we can barter on, over a mug if you've a mind to, we need to be careful?" Freddie nodded, taking David by the hand they made for the alehouse. They had to be watchful under the circumstances.

"This won't take long lad." The 2 men sat and drank down the ale, numbers were tossed around that David did not understand, still, he was happy to sit and watch Freddie at work. An agreement was eventually reached and they shook hands. The man bid the pair farewell after handing over a heavy purse.

"That, young fella, is how you do business. Do you think we could make a fisherman out of you?" He laughed as he clinked his mug against Davids. David was liking the way Freddie had taken him under his wing.

"All done skipper." The other fishermen had entered the inn, sitting down at the table they spoke quietly about grown-up things David presumed.

"No trouble from the law?" asked Freddie.

"Had a quick eye over as they do, glad it's the last one is all I can say." Freddie nodded.

"Aye, won't be taking any more risks that we don't have to I can tell you." They drank up, happy with their day's work done.

"Now young fella, what are we to do with you?" David wasn't sure. He missed Miss Mary and his sister's, Missus too for they were family now. They were closer to home than they had been for a while now, he liked the life of a sailor, he liked Freddie and the men.

"I could stay with you?" David offered. Freddie had a look on his face that told David it wasn't altogether out of the question, this gave him hope.

"Thing of it is young David, if you were a boy of mine and you'd up and gone, I would want to know where and why. Do you think you could trust an old sailor enough to tell me what brought you to Brighton and who you were hiding from?" David shrugged, he would gladly love to tell the truth but in his mind, he could still hear the threats made by that man, threats against Miss Elsbeth and he couldn't have that.

"Can I stay a while longer Mr Freddie Sir?" Freddie sighed, he knew the truth would come, but not yet.

"Course you can son, no rush eh." David smiled with relief, at least this way it would keep them safe he thought.

Billoughby and Tom arrived in Brighton, pulling the map out of his jacket the Inspector studied it carefully.

"Right, we are here." He pointed to a place on the paper.

"We need to be there, seems not too far away would you agree?" Tom nodded, not that he had a clue where they were. They walked on quickly, Tom noticing that for his age, his father had a brisk step on him. They were now on a road named Albion Hill, Reverend Moore's directions seemed to be exact. The sun high in the sky was blazing down on the pair, causing Tom to stop and remove his jacket.

"Getting tired there son?" Asked Billoughby with a smile.

"It's too hot for the time of year, seems even more so being away from the open fields." Billoughby nodded, he too was now feeling uncomfortably warm. It was not his way to remove his jacket, rather keep on to their destination. They checked the street signs with each one that sprung off from the current one.

"Here it is. That's handy, right on the corner" Exclaimed Billoughby.

"About time." Huffed Tom as he quickened to catch up to his father. The Inn stood out on the corner of the road, Tom was quietly pleased that they could also take the chance to get a mug of something refreshing. Inspector Billoughby pushed open the glass-fronted door and went inside. Passing through the room he came to a door. A man was playing a tune on the piano as if to himself as it seemed nobody was listening. Billoughby nodded to him as he made his way to the bar. The inhabitants of the Inn were, it would seem, poorer people. They sat in small groups, lazily supping their woes away. Billoughby approached the man behind the bar.

"Afternoon Sir, I am looking for the proprietor of this establishment. Nothing to get worked up about I might add." The man carefully eyed the pair up.

"That would be me, Mr Boyles. How can I help you Mr?"

"Billoughby, Mr Billoughby. This is my son Tom. I am looking for a man, name of Spires, I heard he has been spending some time here of late."

"Owe you money does he?" Billoughby laughed, shaking his head he placed his cap on the bar and scratched his head.

"Pint Tom?" Tom had sat down by this time, his hair was sodden with the sweat of the heat.

"Yes Sir, best have one before I fall over with heat sickness." Turning back to the man Billoughby shook his head.

"No Sir, he doesn't owe me money, I have a message for him. Quite an important message regarding his son. 2 Pints if you would." The man slackened his stance, the last thing he wanted was trouble with a debt collector, he was happy with the stranger's explanation.

"There you go, Sir, that'll be thruppence. I'll fetch the wife it was her that served the man last. A good week ago now, mind." Billoughby sat down on the bench next to Tom.

"Get that down you son, as warm as the day but will stamp out the thirst." They sat and waited for the man, hoping that they had not had a wasted journey. 5 minutes passed, through the door came a woman drying her hands on the apron she had tied around her waist.

"I hear you fellas are asking after Archie Spires. In here last week he was, not right they had that poor boy out 'til all hours. Still, I told the lad to get off home, Old Archie wasn't best pleased when he came to at closing, kicked up a proper fuss he did."

"Do you remember what the lad looked like?" Asked Tom.

"Small little thing he was, dressed in rags too big for him too, ran off like a scalded cat when I opened the door for him." Billoughby frowned, so the boy was now fending for himself. He could be anywhere by now.

"It would be helpful if you could give me a description of the man in question" The woman went on to describe Spires as Billoughby jotted down the new information.

"You have been very helpful, thank you. Should he emerge again could you do me the favour of trying to keep the child here, I shall leave my details for you to get in touch, it is most important. You will of course be recompensed for your troubles."

"Is the lad in trouble?" The woman seemed concerned, after all, she had sent the child out alone in the dark.

"I'm sure he is better alone than with the gentleman in question." Was all the Inspector could offer.

Billoughby and Tom strolled around the town, they both knew that it would be a miracle if they found David amongst the throngs of people. He was a clever boy, he would not have hung around longer than he had to.

"Where now?" Tom broke the silence that had fallen on the pair. That was the issue, thought the elder man, he had no idea as to 'where now' he was stumped.

"I imagine we have done all we can here son, I don't like to admit defeat but, unless we knock on every door I doubt we will find the lad here today, if at all. My guess would be he's had it away on his heels, he's bright enough to get as far away as he can." Knowing David as well as he did, Tom could not disagree.

Reluctantly they made for the station. All they could hope was that the woman, in time would contact them.

Six

Cate looked around the cottage, her face beaming as she bounced the youngster in her arms.

"See now little one, what your dada has done for us, isn't this a grand home fit for a princess. Oh, Adam, it is just wonderful, I can't believe we will be in our own home tomorrow, I love your ma and pa, sure I do, but this. Well, all I can say is we will be very happy here, of that I'm sure." She kissed her husband on the cheek. Adam had got it right in such a big way. Taking the baby from her arms Adam gave the place a final look over before taking his wife by the hand to make their way back to his mother's house. The walk was a good one, the day was sunny and the birds were singing throughout the countryside, life could not be better thought, Cate. She cast her mind back to when they first saw the cottage, she had not been overly impressed it was true, seeing it today in all its finished glory she felt proud of her husband and brother-in-law for all the hard work they had put into it. Grace, yes she too had played her part making curtains and cushions, bedspreads that matched, even for the little one's room, it was perfect and she loved it.

"What are you thinking there my love?" Cate smiled tenderly, squeezing Adams hand as she did.

"I was thinking how proud I am to call you my husband, the family too. This is so much more than I could have ever dreamt my darling. You have all worked so hard."

"Ah, away you'll have me blushing. I would do anything for you, my love, you know that."

"Do you think your pa and Tom have had any luck today? Seems young David has been away a long time."

Adam shook his head, he had wanted to go with them but his father insisted he stay behind to keep an eye on things.

"I do hope so, although they don't sound the type to hang around in one place from what pa told me. They might not even have the boy,

Because they're a bad lot doesn't make them kidnappers of small children."

"Oh, Lord above. Do you think there could be someone else out there that is snatching children?" Cate looked terrified at this prospect, she had until now felt safe in the knowledge that it was most likely this fella from Canterbury that took David. Adam could have kicked himself, why oh why would he go putting an idea like this into her head.

"You must try not to worry yourself, my love, I don't think there's a child snatcher out there, this was deliberate from what pa says. Young David will turn up I'm sure of it."

They had just about reached the Billoughby cottage when Mary called over to them.

"Hello, out for a walk? It's a nice day for it." Doris was firmly clutching the woman's hand as they crossed the lane.

"We've been over to our new home." Replied Cate excitedly.

"Oh, it must be such a happy time for you. Do you have everything you need? We have lots of items in storage up at the hall from when my parents lived there, aged but still usable."

"That is so kind, everyone has been so generous already. We are short of a few kitchen wares but nothing we can't get along the way." Adam grunted, he was proud and did not like the idea that people may think he could not provide for his family. Cate, on the other hand, saw it as the kind gesture it was intended as.

"Come now young Mr Billoughby, I can't offer a house moving gift?" Mary laughed.

"That is very thoughtful of you Miss Mary, we would be happy to accept such a gift."

"Quite right, Cate dear if you are not busy we could walk over there now, I am happy for you to have a rummage, that way you can pick what is needed."

Adam knew this was an argument he must not start as it would not end in his favour. No, today was to be a calm day to revel in the prospect of all their hard work. Cate briefly called in to see Grace then set off with Mary and Doris.

"Men can be so stubborn dear, it was not meant to offend. I hate to think of these things going to waste when they are very practical items."

"Do you have a lot of things saved from your parents days at the hall?"

"Far too many, most of them we stored when the children came, not that any breakages would be a problem but the house was incredibly cluttered. It seemed practical to lighten the space as it were. Children need to feel they can roam around their home without worrying they may bump into a thing, don't you agree?"

"I do, my ma had glass trinkets all over the place, scared to the bone I was of knocking them over, them being her pride and joy." Cate laughed at the memory she had forgotten about.

"Doris agrees too, don't you, my little angel." Doris had no idea what the 2 grown-ups were talking about, yet nodded all the same.

"Do you have an idea of what time Inspector Billoughby will be returning?" Maty's voice was hushed now as if to conceal her question from the child's ears. Cate shook her head, mindful of not speaking out of turn.

"It will be tonight by all accounts. How is Mrs Stanhope bearing up, she must be ay her witts end with the worry of it all."

"Yes, the poor woman can barely concentrate on a thing, why, twice this week I have taken the little ones back to stay at the farm in the hope that she can get some rest. Blames herself, of course, heaven knows why as nobody could have foreseen this."

"I hate to think of her all alone in that big house." Mary shrugged.

"She daren't stay with us for fear that David may come back and find the house empty." They walked on quietly, Mary hoping that the Inspector would return with good news, Cate thinking over what her husband had said.

"Afternoon ladies."

"Reverend, how lovely to see you. How are you?"

"I am very well thank you, Mary, Young Daisy has a guest from London, I thought it would be polite to give them some time to catch up. Cate, I don't imagine the Inspector has arrived back from Brighton as yet?" Cate shook her head.

"This evening, or so I have heard Reverend."

"You could accompany us to the hall Reverend, a spot of tea perhaps?" Reverend Moore walked alongside the ladies, chattering about various events he was hoping to hold in the lead up to harvest.

"Miss Mary, I have an idea," Cate interjected amid the Reverend's mumblings.

"What would that be dear?" Cate had the sudden thought, now that she had their attention she wondered if it was too forward a proposal.

"Don't be bashful dear."

"You mentioned the number of spare items you have stored, I thought, it is only a thought mind. What about a sale of unwanted items? It would raise some needed money for the church and, for the causes that Reverend Moore is involved with." Mary pursed her lips as she thought about the suggestion.

"Reverend, what do you think? Would that be an acceptable thing to do?"

"Goodness, that is a jolly good idea. No family heirlooms mind you, things that are affordable to the community would be marvellous. Cate, you are a wonder." Cate grinned from ear to ear, pleased that her suggestion had not been ridiculed.

"Would you be interested in arranging such a thing Cate, as it was your idea? I could help sort through what we are happy to donate, with the care of the children I could not commit to being on hand to carry out the organising of the event. Would it be too much trouble for you do you think?"

"I would be happy to arrange it, with your permission, of course, Reverend."

"That's settled, now for tea." Mary pushed open the heavy door to the hall.

"Doris dear, go wash your hands and come back to the kitchen for a drink. Elsbeth, are you here dear?" she called.

"In the parlour Mary." Came the reply. The trio went into the parlour.

"I hope you don't mind my dear, we have a few guests." Elsbeth shook her head, she had the baby cradled in her arms.

"Any news?" Her question was directed to Cate, a hopeful expression on her face.

"I'm sorry Ma'am, no news as yet."

"As I imagined. Please, sit. I shall put the little one down, she seems to have tired of my conversation and fallen asleep." Mary left the room to make the tea, joined by Doris.

"Would you like to help?" Doris nodded, she liked helping Miss Mary in the kitchen if only to set out cups on the tray, it made her feel grown-up.

"You have been practising, that is very good dear one. Would you like to pour the milk into that jug?"

Again Doris nodded, the milk urn was heavy but she did not let that deter her efforts, spilling only a small drop she was pleased with her pouring.

"Well done my angel, you did that perfectly. Now, which cake shall we have, would you like to choose?" Doris knew which cake she would like, the one that had raspberry jam inside and a dusting of sweet sugar on top. Instead, she chose the fruit cake, grown-ups like fruit cake and today she was being a grown-up. Mary smiled at her choice.

"Pop along and hold the door open for me, there's a dear." Once Doris left the kitchen, Mary placed a small piece of cake with raspberry jam on the tea tray next to the fruit cake. How sweet the child had chosen for others above herself, surely deserves a reward. When Mary placed the tray on the table, Doris grinned. Miss Mary must be magic she thought as she had not asked for the cake. Reverend Moore was busy telling Elsbeth about the plan to raise monies for the church. Mary could see by the woman's expression that this news was not as well-received as she had hoped it would be.

"Did you know about this Mary?" Her tone was flat as she stared at her sister-in-law.

"I did, in fact, I think it is a marvellous idea, you can get rid of some items that are not of use and take up space and, the church funds will benefit."

"I think a private word." Replied Elsbeth as she left the room.

"Oh, Miss I am that sorry, I did not mean to cause you a problem." Cate was mortified at Mrs Stanhope's reaction. Mary shook her head.

"Don't worry dear, it has not been a happy time for Mrs Stanhope since David and I really should have gotten her permission first." Mary joined Elsbeth in the kitchen.

"Close the door." Commanded the woman, she was rigid in her stance as Mary shut the kitchen door.

"Elsbeth, can I."

"Am I mistaken in the fact that the house and its belongings were left in my sole ownership, have I not been generous in my letting you stay here and how am I repaid? You would give everything away behind my back with not so much as a backward glance at the woman that took you in." Mary was shocked at the outrage coming from this ordinarily pleasant woman. She knew that all was not well because of the boy, but this, this was unnecessary in every sense of the word.

"I shall forgive your rudeness this once, I know you are suffering terribly over the loss of the young Master David." For the second time in as many minutes, Elsbeth cut her comments short.

"*YOU* WILL FORGIVE *ME*! How dare you, and how dare you refer to it as a loss, he is not dead. It is not for you to decide what I shall do with articles from this house." Mary could feel her face getting hotter by the second, a tear stung as it dropped over her eyelid. There was little point continuing with this conversation, not now. Mary pulled open the door, her footsteps echoing in the hall followed by a large thud as she slammed the main door to the house behind her.

In the parlour, the Reverend and Cate fell into an awkward silence. Elsbeth did not return to the parlour, after some 20 minutes the pair took their leave. Doris sat alone, not daring to touch the appealing slice of cake.

"And then, we could hear Mrs Stanhope screaming at poor Miss Mary, Miss Mary left and slammed the door." Cate took another gulp of her tea. Grace was shocked, she knew Cate well enough to know the girl would not have embellished the story in any way, that and Reverend Moore backed it up.

"She is under an awful lot of pressure at the moment, still, Mary must be feeling terrible. Maybe I should go over and see that she is okay." Grace already had her scarf in hand, ready to make her way over to find out about Mary's well-being.

"I shall accompany you Mrs Billoughby, I must make sure that Daisy and her guest are comfortable."

"Heavens, I completely forgot in all the fuss, they are coming for supper," Grace said as she threw her hands into the air.

"I will start supper ma, don't you worry about it. Please give my apologies to Miss Mary, I never meant to get her into such a ruck." Grace tucked her scarf around her head.

"If Mr Billoughby gets back before I do please explain that I will be as quick as I can. Make Daisy and her guest comfortable, I hope not to be too long. Reverend, you are coming back to join us for supper?" Reverend Moore was nodding his head, not a man to pass up a supper invitation.

"That is most kind of you, yes, thank you. I shall see you soon dear girl and please try not to worry about the whole thing, it will sort itself out I am sure."

Robert opened the farmhouse door. He did not look happy.

"Can't get no sense out of her, she went out full of the joys, came back in tears she did. I tried to get to what upset her so, maybe you will have more luck Grace." Grace tapped gently on the bedroom door.

"Mary dear, Mary it's Grace, can I come in?" From inside the room, Grace could hear a muffled reply followed by the sound of Mary blowing her nose. She pushed the door open to see Mary peering into the mirror in an attempt to wipe the tears away.

"Oh, my dear woman. Come here, sit beside me and tell me what has happened." Mary poured out the humiliating berating that had been given to her up at the hall as Grace shook her head in disbelief. Robert stood at the door with tea, he listened quietly, his anger swelling inside.

"Drink this, my love. Grace, tea?" Grace took the 2 mugs from the visibly angry man.

"I've got a mind to go over there." He hissed. Mary looked up startled.

"Please don't, I would rather put the whole sorry argument behind us. She did not mean to be so harsh, I know this. Elsbeth has suffered so many losses, she was likely to snap at some point."

"That is no excuse, my love, she cannot talk to you in that way, it is disgraceful. That was your family home and like it or not you have a claim to take whatever you see fit to take. It belonged to your parents, not hers. Hell Mary, she was only married to your brother a month or so." Mary began to sob again, Grace had never seen the once stoic woman so distressed and it pained her. Robert left the 2 women alone, he paced the floor of the kitchen watched by a confused Sal and Mary's dogs. Sal's eyes followed him as he went back and forth. He leant to stroke the trio as he contemplated what to do. His heart told him to go over to the hall and give that woman a piece of his mind, that would not, however, please his wife.

"Come by you 3." He decided instead to walk off his frustration.

"You don't think he has gone over there?" Grace shook her head, for she knew that this man would do anything for Mary, even if it meant biting his lip.

"I wouldn't blame him if he did dear, but no, maybe he's done what Mr Billoughby does on these such times and taken a walk."

"You must have a lot to do Grace, what with the youngsters moving tomorrow. Please don't let a silly, hysterical woman keep you."

"Now Mary, we both know that you are neither of these things, I shall stay until I am happy that you are feeling better." Grace drank her tea. In her mind, she knew what she was going to do. After all, Mary had not told *her* not to go over to the hall.

"Why don't you and Robert come to ours for supper dear, the more company the better."

"That is so kind of you Grace, if I'm honest I don't feel much in the mood for company, I feel tired, more than I ever have before." Grace could imagine, the woman never cried and it must have knocked the stuffing from her.

"If you change your mind dear we will be sitting down a little after 7. Think about it will you?" They heard the door open and close, Robert appeared in the room.

"How are you feeling, love?" Mary smiled weakly at her husband, bless this man for she was sure he hadn't bargained on a wailing wife when he took her on.

"Much better thank you, my love. Grace invited us to eat with them at the cottage if you would like to?"

"I think that would do you the world of good. Thank you, Grace, shall we bring anything?"

"No dear, your selves is more than enough. Have a little nap Mary and we shall see you at 7." She patted the woman fondly on the shoulder.

Elsbeth opened the door, she looked as red-faced and exhausted as Mary had.

"Grace, this is a surprise. What can I do for you?" Unlike other occasions, Elsbeth did not invite Grace into the house. Now that she was there, Grace wasn't quite sure what she was going to say. A mild-mannered woman and yet, she felt, for the first time in a long time the anger rise inside her chest. She swallowed as if to shift the ball that was between her ribs.

"Grace?"

"Might I come in?"

"Will this take long, I have things to attend to." Grace shifted on her feet, this was not going to be an easy conversation by any stretch of the imagination.

"I shouldn't think so. I have had cause to pay a visit to Mary." Elsbeth stepped back.

"I hardly feel this is of your concern, I would not have had you down as a village gossip Grace." Grace breathed in slowly, this was not the same woman that had spent pleasant afternoons with, this was a bitter woman standing before her now.

"I am neither gossip nor a person to get in the middle of a family dispute. I call here as a friend, to both you and Mary. Surely you can see how upset this has made the poor woman?"

"Are my feelings not important too? Does it not occur to Mary that she ought to have sought my permission when offering out the contents of my home?"

"A home that was once her own. Mary had lived all her life in this house with her family, her family home Elsbeth, does that mean nothing to you?" Elsbeth bit down hard on her lip, she had not the mental energy for this tonight.

"If, and I say if, the family had wanted Mary to have all of this, they would have left it to her. Her brother would have left it to her, he did not. I have no objection to raising money for a worthy cause, I will not tolerate a partial stranger coming into my home with the expectation that I will simply hand over whatever takes their fancy. That is all I have to say on the matter Grace, a matter, I might remind you that has absolutely nothing to do with you." Grace jumped back as the large door slammed shut in her face.

Doris stood at the bottom of the stairs in silence clutching a ragged old bear.

"Doris dear, did you need something?" The child shook her head and returned upstairs to her room. Sitting on the cot she cradled the old toy in her arms, stroking the tatty fur that was now fading with age. She wished David was here, he would know what to do.

Grace arrived back at the cottage, it hadn't taken her as long as normally would the walk from the hall. Fuelled by the anger that pumped around inside her. She stood outside breathing in the air, the last thing she wanted was to go inside raging. She barely heard the sound of the cart as it clip-clopped down the lane toward her.

"What is ma doing?" asked a bemused Tom.

"Son, the day I understand your mother will be the day St Peter himself whispers in my ear and maybe not even then I'm sure."

"Ma?" Grace spun around, surprised at the sight of her husband and son.

"Goodness, I didn't realise you were there. Hello Mr Nash."

"Evening Mrs Billoughby. Taking in a breath I see." Mr Nash tipped his hat and trotted on, Tom and Billoughby waving their thanks.

"Is everything well, my love?" Billoughby knew Grace well enough to know that something was most definitely not well. Tom kissed his mother on the cheek as he made for the door.

"Wait, Tom. I need to speak alone with you." Turning to her husband Grace stared into his eyes.

"Did you have the conversation with Tom, is it cleared up?" Billoughby frowned, not like his Grace to get involved in these matters.

"I did, not cleared up as yet. Whatever is the matter, my love."

"Tom, you will answer me a question, I am in no mind to hear lies or silence. This is not a game, it needs settling once and for good." Tom had no idea what his ma was talking about, was it the Thompson girl, had she said something?

"If I can ma."

"You can and you will." Tom had never seen his mother angry, for that matter, Billoughby hadn't in all their years of marriage.

"Gracie, love can we talk about this just you and me?" Grace shook her head.

"I never interfere Milton, but I feel I must. Tom, you will tell me now why you went to the hall on the day before David's going missing. You will not lie to me, regardless of the reason, do you understand?" Tom had never lied to his mother, this had put him in an awkward position and no mistake.

"Ma, what has happened? Have you heard something?"

"I won't ask again Tom, enough going on in this village without hearing tales of how your father has failed to question you, his son that was seen up there with no explanation. I will have that explanation now Tom."

Billoughby stared at Grace, so there was already talk of Tom being over there!

"Tom?" Tom stared at his feet, what was he to do.

"We are friends, that's all."

"What do you mean, friends? What business does the woman have being friends with a boy of your age?"

"I can have friends mother, I am not a child." Tom was getting irritated at the line of questioning, it was nobody's business but his.

"If you have a friend then why did you take such a time to say why you were there?"

"I was not there as such, I called, I did not go in and I left. That is all." Tom stomped off into the house leaving his mother and father speechless on the path outside.

"I have finished supper ma." Cate was busy readying the table when Grace and Milton came through.

"Thank you, dear, oh that was a good idea, we may have a little more company than first thought. Yes, this will do nicely."

"How was Mary?" Billoughby was confused and rightly so.

"What has happened woman, we have been gone a day and it would appear the devil has taken hold since our departure." Cate made herself busy in the other room, she could sense this day not brightening up any.

Grace proceeded to tell her husband about the going's on of the day at the hall, she also told of how Sally had mentioned to Mrs Thompson that Tom had been whispering with Elsbeth at the hall yet he had not been asked to explain his actions.

"It's all too much Milton, I was wrong to stop you questioning Tom. I stand fast that he had nothing to do with the boy's disappearance but I will not have idle gossip about our family. You have no idea the kind of day we have had." Billoughby placed his arm around his distressed wife's shoulder.

"Come inside my love, we will talk about it all later when the house is quieter. You say we have guests for supper, let's not spoil it with talk of upset, I'm quite looking forward to seeing the visitor that Daisy will bring."

When they entered the parlour, Tom was busy going over the plans with his brother for the next day's move.

"Bright and early brother, the sooner we start, the sooner Cate can get things settled."

"Is that your bright and early, or my bright and early?" Joked Adam, for he knew that to Tom it would most likely mean as the birds woke, Adam had gotten used to the new and leisurely lifestyle that came with the countryside.

"My bright and early. Tell me, Adam, have you decided what you will do with yourself, for a living?" Adam scratched his head.

"I imagine I will go into farming, it's about the only steady thing around here."

"I hear the smithy is to retire soon, with no family to pass it down to would that be something you might consider?" Adam's face perked up, this was news to him and he was handy with metal, he had to be given the job he had helped complete on the liner.

"You know, I may just be interested in that line of work. In fact, I shall go over tomorrow when we're done at the cottage and have a word with the old fella. Thank you brother, you are definitely the smart one of us 2." Tom smiled, glad that he could spark a possible interest for his kin. The door opened, Daisy and Julian Richardson entered the parlour. Daisy gripped tightly onto his arm.

"This is Mr Richardson, from London." She gushed as if showing off a prized possession.

"Please, call me Julian. It is so very nice of you to invite us at such short notice." Daisy made her way into the kitchen, she was eager to share her news with Grace and Billoughby. The Reverend was busy unloading a basket of goodies they had brought along.

"Fine slab of cheese there Reverend, are you sure we won't be leaving your pantry short with all of these offering's?" The Reverend shook his head, his toothy grin visible.

"Not a problem Mrs Billoughby, I have at least 2 of these great lumps left to get me through the winter months. No, I could not have turned up empty-handed, not the done thing at all." Daisy was standing by the table, her patience waning somewhat as the Reverend continued to chatter about his pantry and its contents.

"Daisy, my dear, how are you? Is your visitor here?"

"He is Mrs Billoughby, sitting in the parlour. I wanted to tell you both, well the 3 of you really, of my exciting news." Grace put the plates down and wiped her hands.

"Come on then girl, let's hear it."

"Julian, that is, Mr Richardson has asked me to consider a position at the palace, you know, Buckingham Palace where the King lives. I was that worried he might propose that I didn't think for a minute it would be a job offer, and me a woman. Oh, isn't it an exciting opportunity Inspector?"

The trio looked stunned, they too had expected a wedding, not a job offer. They had all grown extremely fond of the young woman in the time she had been amongst them, part of the family she was.

"Well, say something, anybody. Is it not a grand step-up for a girl like me?" The Inspector cleared his throat.

"Daisy, is that what you want?" Daisy shrugged, if it meant being closer to her Julian it was.

"Isn't it a great opportunity Inspector?"

"My dear, are you not happy here?" Asked Grace, Grace knew that quietly Daisy would rather have had the marriage opportunity.

"I am extremely happy here Mrs Billoughby. You have all been as close as a family could be, if I am to be taken seriously in my work I cannot pass this up, it's a chance of a lifetime and would do so much for the women in the constabulary would it not?" They were interrupted by the knock at the back door.

"Oh, good. This must be Mary and Robert. Now, let's try to keep the conversation light for Mary's sake shall we." Said Grace as she pulled the door open.

"How lovely that you were able to make it, please come in." Robert and Mary joined the small group in the parlour, keen to hear about the big move in the morning.

"You must let us know if you need any help with anything, we would be more than happy to help." Offered Mary.

"You are very kind Miss Mary, I think we have everything ready to go." Cate paused, her expression changing as a thought occurred to her.

"Oh, there is something, a big something as it happens." She turned to Adam, he, in turn, shook his head, he had no idea what the 'thing' was.

"Little one, we have not organised anyone to have the little one while we are busy with the moving."

"Blimey, that is true."

"Then I shall consider that my day if it's all the same to you, dear?" Robert was happy enough that his dear wife would have something to keep her mind busy.

"Are you quite sure Miss Mary?" Mary nodded, she liked the company of children.

"It will be my pleasure dear girl."

The evening went on to be a very nice one, Cate's huge Irish stew went down a treat with the accompaniment of fresh bread and ale. Mary left a happier woman than the one that arrived, promising to return first thing in the morning to take the child for the day. Daisy and Mr Richardson escorted a slightly worse for wear Reverend Moore back to the rectory.

"We shall speak tomorrow Miss." Called Billoughby, to Daisy as they left.

Grace sat in bed, her cup of tea resting on her raised knee under the cover. She had enjoyed the impromptu supper party, it had been a while since the house had been that full. She watched Billoughby as he carefully folded his trousers, hanging them over the back of the chair. He was a good husband, she considered herself fortunate in every way that they had the life they did. The tall, still handsome man glided into bed next to his wife.

"Well now Mrs Billoughby, I noticed you had a fair few mugs of ale tonight and, if memory serves me, ale makes you a little friskier than usual." Grace chuckled, never one to miss a trick this man of mine, she thought as she placed her cup on the table beside her. He laughed as his big strong arms wrapped themselves around her, kissing this wonderful woman with the passion that he kept only for her. Grace almost felt her breath taken away at the sudden movements he made to position her just so.

Elsbeth was striding the large almost empty corridors in the Hall. Her mind whirring in fury over the day's events. At one point she had mused to herself that maybe she had been too harsh, this had quickly turned to indignation when she recalled the way that the trio had simply assumed they could do as they pleased. It was true to say that they would think the way she reacted to be out of character, maybe she was, this had been a Lord awful year what with one thing and another. She stopped at the door of the nursery, the 2 children slept quietly now. The soft, steady sounds of their breathing seemed to steady her thoughts for a while.

"Where are you, David?" She whispered into the quiet night. Closing the door gently, Elsbeth made her way down the stairs. In the kitchen, she began preparing the table for the next morning's breakfast when she heard the quiet tap on the door.

"Who's there?" She called as quietly as she could.

"It's me." Came the reply.

Opening the heavy door she smiled, it had been too long and arduous a day not to.

"Not disturbing you am I?"

"Not at all, I was about to have a hot drink. Won't you join me?"

"That would be welcome, thank you. It's a fair chilly wind creeping up out there. I would say Summer is coming to a close."

"I dare say the ground will be happy with that, it has not rained for such a long time now."

The pair picked up their mugs as Elsbeth led the way upstairs to the warmth of her room with its hearty fire radiating heat.

Seven

David had enjoyed his day, he had happily helped where he could which had pleased the Captain no end.

"Time you were catching up on some sleep young 'en. You did well today." He smiled at the man, trying to stifle a yawn as he did so.

"Thank you, Sir, it was fun. What are we doing in the morning?" Freddie scratched his head, a habit David had come to recognise.

"I'm thinking we might take the old girl on a slow wave back to Brighton, not decided yet. What about you Master David, where do you have a mind to go?" David felt very grown-up, that the Captain would ask him.

Freddie continued as he pulled off his boots and rubbed his feet.

"We could try to find your Missus if you've got a mind to?" David would dearly have loved to go back to the Hall, he missed his sisters, he missed Miss Mary and Miss Elsbeth. What of the man that took him? Would he go back and carry out his threat?

"You're the boss, Sir, I reckon I go where you go." Freddie shrugged, would he ever get the truth of where this little chap had come from?

"Sleep, nipper. We'll work it out in the morning."

Archie lurched over to the bar, slamming his mug on the surface he gestured for another refill. The man playing the piano stopped. He stared at the fella for a short time before approaching.

"Archie is your name?" Archie spun around in his seat.

"And who wants to know?" He jeered.

"Might have some information for you if you are him, Go back to playing the ivories if you ain't."

"What'll it cost me and is it worth the price?" The man grinned showing his gums, 2 teeth remaining in his mouth.

"Pint of the landlords best is what it'll cost you, I'm no thief."

"Let's hear it then and if it is useful, and only if, I will get you that pint." The man went on to tell Archie about the men that came from the South, he told that he thought they might be the law, that they were looking for a youngster that had been snatched. Archie's face began to lose its colour as the man talked on. The woman behind the bar scowled at the piano player.

"Time you went home, I'll not be serving you anymore this night I can tell you. You want to pay no mind to that one Mr, he tells the same tale to anyone he thinks will buy him a pint."

"It's true, as I live and breath fella."

"Go on, get off with you and peddle your stories somewhere else." Archie was not the brightest of men luckily for the woman.

"Tells anyone the same you say?"

"He does that, been telling that same tale for nigh on 20 years and all to get a pint out of poor hardworking and honest blokes like yourself," Archie smirked, straightened his coat and joined his accomplice at the table.

"Likes me, that one." He said as he winked over to the woman.

"Filthy wretches." She whispered under her breath.

It wasn't until the pair left the Inn that they noticed the old man was still waiting outside.

"Tried to make a fool out of me Mr?" The man cowered back at seeing the enormity of Archie's companion.

"Not me Sir, I never would. She be telling you an untruth, I don't rightly know why but she's lied to you. Fella's came yesterday or was it today, anyhow, they were looking for you. Said you done off with a youngster or some such story. She said she helped the young 'en getaway while you were dozing."

Archie stared at the old man, he had no reason to wait, he had no reason to make a thing up that he knew nothing about.

"Here, what did these fella's look like?" The man leant forward and described Billoughby and Tom.

"Pay the man a shilling Scrapper."

The woman in the bar thought it best to send her message the following day. She placed the call from the post office to Joseph's home. Joseph agreed to get the message to Billoughby as quickly as he could. It came as no surprise to the Inspector that the child was no longer with the pair. The woman had relayed that the men had rooms in the town, she gave a good deal of information in her short call. Joseph's man asked if he should take a message back.

"Tell Dr, here, I shall write a note." Billoughby ushered the man in and quickly scribbled a note for his friend.

"Please give Dr Lyons my regards and this note." Tom watched from the table at the exchange of information.

"No news of David?"

"Nothing, the 2 fella's are still in Brighton, it would seem they too are still looking for the boy. You are up early today son, getting ready for the big move?" Tom nodded, he hadn't slept much the previous night.

"Trying to waken that brother of mine is a lost cause, he wants to start early but will not stir." He laughed.

"About your conversation with your Ma last night, is there anything else you want to tell me?" Tom shook his head.

"No Pa, not as I can think." Billoughby wasn't going to push this at the moment, he would if he had to but not this day.

"Getting back to David, is it worth going back over there? The lad could be anywhere by now. What do you think son?" Tom finished down his tea, his face scrunched as he thought about the question.

"If you ask me Pa, I think the lad will try to make for home. Going back over there is a risky thing if you believe what the fella in Canterbury told you. You might get more trouble than you bargain for."

"Aye, could have a point. Right, let's see if we can wake your brother. Mary will be along soon enough to pick the baby up."

Mary was in heaven at the farm. She so loved the children, all children so it was a blessing that Cate had allowed her to take the child for the day.

"Imagine my love, had we had our own, you would have made the perfect mother." It was a sadness that often crept over Robert when he watched his wife with the little ones. How cruel could life be and yet what a blessing that they found each other again after all the time that had gone in between?

Mary simply smiled, she chose not to dwell on what might have been, it was too painful and she was happy with her lot.

"Are you not just a darling child? Yes, you are." She cooed at the baby, who in return stared back with her bright inquisitive eyes.

"I best get on, short of Tom today. If you need anything give me a shout my love." He kissed his wife on the forehead and waved to the baby.

"Don't work too hard dear, I shall call you for lunch." Mary lay the child back in her basket as she set about tidying the breakfast dishes. Singing softly as she did so until the child fell into a contented sleep. Yes, Mary was happy.

"Time we made a move Captain, that local constabulary lot keep eyeing us up." Freddie could not agree more. They had been lucky yesterday when they offloaded the cargo, small as it was and well hidden to boot. No reason to get their faces known, definitely time to move on.

"I thought we might head off down the coastline a bit, we keep saying a visit to Hythe or thereabouts would make a change. What say you?" The fisherman nodded.

"Change is as good in my book. Any reason Skipper or we testing the water so to speak?" Freddie shrugged.

"I've got a feeling we should, no rhyme or reason." David slept on that morning, the crew had eaten at the Inn felt no haste to awaken the young boy.

"You're the Captain, we'll ready the old girl." Freddie made his way to the cabin, he watched the young boy as he slept peacefully and undisturbed by the clatter of the men outside. He had studied the boy carefully over the time they had him aboard, he had a tidy well-groomed underlying look about him, his manners, although he tried to hide it, had been refined in a way that a street urchin would not. No, there was more to the lad than he was letting on. Somebody somewhere was missing this child. He aimed to get the boy home. It did not take long for the small vessel to be on its way, the air was damp. Rain was most certainly on its way.

Reverend Moore was busy writing in his journal when Daisy finally appeared. He looked up at the bright-faced woman as she placed a cup of tea on his desk.

"You have said your goodbye's my dear?"

"For now, I feel quite the fool Reverend." Tobias placed his pen on the book, his face showing her that he did not quite understand the remark.

"I thought he was going to propose, there I was all nervous about how I would accept and he offers me a job."

"Sit down my dear. Did you want him to propose, I mean, you have not known each other for very long?"

"I want to do well in my work, I do, it's just."

"Come, come dear. What is it?"

"Women will never get very far in any profession, is it my right as a woman to turn down a position that could change this, on the other hand, what if I fail thus giving people the opinion that they were right all along to not engage a woman in such a role?" Tobias laughed, Daisy frowned at the usually kind Reverend.

"You find my conundrum amusing Reverend?" Taking her hand he shook his head.

"No my dear, I find your lack of confidence in yourself bewildering. Do you think for a moment that the Inspector would have kept you around if he thought you were not up to the tasks he sets you, tasks that I might add you carry out extremely well?" Daisy sat back in the chair, it was true that Billoughby did not suffer fools gladly.

"Oh, do tell me what to do Reverend before I burst with over-thinking the thing."

"I would selfishly say not to go, for I have become accustomed to your company. Unselfish, then it is clear. You must go and plant your feet firmly for women everywhere. Geraldine would gladly welcome you into her home until such a time that you are ready to start your own I am sure. She would also very likely champion you on." Daisy nodded, he had his funny ways and yet he always spoke truthfully and justly.

"And of marriage? Shall I simply put that out of my mind?"

"When the time is right it will happen, my dear, you will know when that time is. When are they expecting your answer?"

"Within the fortnight. I will write to Geraldine today. I shall take the position. There, that's settled, now I have only to speak with the Inspector." Daisy left the room to attend to her tasks. Tobias felt happy for the woman, sad that he would miss her.

Adam and Tom were taking the last pieces of heavy furniture into the cottage when Sally came by, her arms laden with a basket of fresh-smelling treats.

"Mrs at the Hall asked me to drop these around, she thought you might be hungry."

"Blimey, that's awful big of her considering the ructions yesterday. Cate's inside Sally if you want to go in before we get stuck."

"What ructions are these Cate? Here you are my girl, from the Missus at the Hall."

"Oh, you haven't heard? She fair tore the hide off just about everyone she came across did Mrs Stanhope."

"No! She never did?"

"As I live and breath she did. Had poor Miss Mary in tears so she did, Ma was spitting fire when she came back from there. Didn't leave me out neither. I tell you, Sally, I don't know what's got into the woman so I don't." Sally was shocked, she had known Elsbeth a long time and had never in all that time heard such a thing.

"Now Cate, the woman has a lot on her plate, not our place to spread gossip about her."

"Adam, my love, I am not spreading gossip if I was party to the outburst, which I was."

"Still gossip in my book, her not here to defend herself." Added Tom curtly.

"Ooh, Tom my dear, are we carrying a torch for the Lady of the manner?" Tom bit his lip.

"Now Sally, that's a ridiculous notion and no mistake. She's twice Tom's age if not more." Laughed Adam.

"Tell me this then if you can, what was your brother doing up at the big house the day before the little lad went missing?" Sally placed her hands on her hips in a triumphant stance.

"None of your business is what." Spat back, Tom.

"And I'll thank you not to go spreading such tales especially to my mother."

"Saw what I saw, as I said to Grace. If we are questioned, so should you be."

"Come along you 2, let's not have a bad feeling on the first day in our new home." Cate tried to smooth things over, she could tell things could very quickly escalate at this rate.

"Tea, anyone. Oh, and cake, I see cake in the basket that Sally's brought."

Tom took his tea outside, what was it with a small community that they felt they had the right to know everything about everybody?

"Pay no mind to her Tom, she means nothing by it." Cate offered the plate with a slice of cake tempting him to accept the white flag.

"She wouldn't be so smug if Mrs Stanhope knew that her going's on were being used around the village as Sally's topic of gossip. Be out on her ear she would and she knows it."

"Still, even you have to admit that your visits over there are bound to set tongues a-wagging. Even more so once the Thompson girl moves in on Monday." Tom stared up at his sister-in-law.

"What do you mean by that? Why would she be moving in at the Hall?" Cate's face flushed hot.

"Didn't you know? Mrs Stanhope has taken her on as a housemaid, kitchen help. She wants her to live-in to help with the children. Why is all of this so important to you Tom?" Tom shrugged.

"It isn't." Turning away from Cate he bit into the cake and said nothing more.

Elsbeth was stumped. Doris had not spoken a word to her all day, even when she purposely misread the storybook. This was a game they played, Elsbeth would misread and Doris would giggle then correct her. Not so today, she simply stared out of the window in silence.

"What do you think we will have for supper dear?" Silence.

"Would you like to choose?" Still not a word. Elsbeth, exasperated by her efforts left the child to play quietly with her toy.

"What of you little Miss, do you have any ideas on supper?" She asked the baby that lay comfortably in her arms. The infant simply gurgled, yawned then closed her eyes. She lay the child back in her crib, stroking the soft warm hair that had begun to grow steadily as the weeks rolled on.

"Sleep well, dearest child." Muttered the woman as she left the room. Back in the parlour, Doris sat rocking her tatty old toy wondering what had made the Missus so cross. Was she to expect a walloping as her mother had in the past when she had been angry? Would the Missus simply send her away as maybe she had with David?

"Doris, come along dear your supper is ready." Doris headed for the kitchen, easing herself carefully up into the chair she placed her faithful old bear on the table beside the cutlery.

"My dearest child, do we imagine your bear would be more comfortable on your cot? He is a little dirty to have on the table don't you think?" The child slid the bear from the table, tucking it onto her lap out of sight.

"There now, isn't this better?" Doris nodded although she did not agree, Scruffy liked to sit on the table, he could watch over Doris warning her of any whacks headed her way.

Try as she might, Elsbeth could not engage the child in conversations of any type.

"I thought it might be fun if we went on a small trip, would you like that Doris? I have been meaning to visit cousin Renton, he is not my cousin as such, cousin of my departed husband you see. You met them at the wedding, do you recall? Not important I agree, they mentioned it would be convenient this coming week. Yes, we shall visit. You will find their children pleasant company I am sure." Elsbeth was rambling, what's more, she knew it! Doris was having very different thoughts, the Missus was going to take her away and not bring her back.

Cate finally settled Maisy down to sleep. It had been a long day for all of them.

"Do you like our new home Mrs Billoughby?" She smiled a tired, contented smile to Adam.

"It is perfect my lovely, perfect and ours. Maybe one day my parents could visit, we have the space now?"

"Whatever makes you happy my love. Time to sleep I think, it has been a full-on day has it not?"

Cate yawned, she loved her husband and their daughter, this beautifully quaint cottage.

"It has, I hope poor Tom gets some decent sleep tonight. He has worked ever so hard, you both have. A strange conversation I had with him today, he was ever so defensive about Mrs Stanhope. I can't help but feel there is something not quite as it should be there. Adam? Adam, what do you think?"

Adam was asleep, Cate rolled over as she tucked herself up against him. He let out a sigh in the quiet of the night. Cate lay pondering the talk she had with Tom, surely she was mistaken for what other reason would he have to keep sneaking over to the Hall? Then it dawned on the young woman, of course, Tom must be doing some work on the quiet and why not. If he could make an extra few shillings good luck to the man. Satisfied with her conclusion Cate drifted off to sleep. The newly thatched roof did the young family proud that night for as they slept the first rain in months began to fall in the English countryside marking the end of the 1911 heatwave.

"Mary, Mary look!" Robert was jumping with glee when he opened the drapes that morning. Mary, bleary-eyed had no idea what was going on or, why her husband was prancing around the room in his undergarments.

"What? What has happened?" Asked the still half-asleep woman. Robert almost skipped over to his wife who was trying to get her bearings on the bed. Kissing her full on the mouth then taking her hand as he led her to the window.

"See! It's raining, there may be hope for those crops yet. Mind, they will be later than they should be but, Mary, don't you see? The drought could be over at last." Mary smiled, there were not many people she knew would be happy to see rain. For most, the hot weather had been an extended Summer, chances to go to the seaside and bask in the rays, for others it had proved unbearable in that it was often uncomfortable but for folk like Robert in the farming business it had been dreadful. The fields which had been ablaze under the unrelenting heat, ruining what little crops had managed to grow thus sinking some farming families into financial ruin were all too fresh in their minds.

"Do you think it is possible to save some of the harvests?" Robert shook his head.

"It has to be worth a try. We are lucky mind you, once we managed to dig out the trench at the river it did help to soak the land. Not like most, higher up with no chance of getting water to the crops. That's farming, either too high ground in Summer or too low in the rainy seasons."

"Yes, I felt ever so sad for the Fisher's, not only did they lose the crops to that dreadful fire but their home to the lenders. What a sorry business that was." Robert thought back to the day when the Fisher's blaze took hold, try as they might the locals who rallied to help could not outrun the flames, all they could do in the end was to watch the whole lot shrivel up in flames. They were not the only one's to suffer, 3 other local farms suffered similar losses, luckily they were able to survive on the pastoral stock they had. Still, a hefty blow regardless.

"Look, here comes Tom. Best get myself clothed and down to breakfast. Lots to do Mary, lots to do."

And with that, he was gone. Mary sat back on the bed, what a year it has been she thought. Elsbeth, what should she do regarding Elsbeth? Mary could well imagine the toll of losing David in such a way was causing her sister-in-law a great upset, as it was for her too. Should she go to the Hall and try to mend this before it got out of hand? They had built such a good relationship in the time they had known each other, it would be a great sorrow to lose the friendship over something so insignificant would it not? Mary had made a decision, she would go over to mend this particular fence. If Elsbeth refused to see it as a silly fuss over nothing, well at least Mary could say she tried.

"Doris, are you ready, do you have your bear? We have to leave dear, the coach is here. Esther, can you please hurry the child along, we do not want to miss our train." Esther ran up the stairs, returning quickly holding the child's hand in her's.

"Ah, there you are. Are you excited?" Doris looked at the floor. Esther wondered why the little girl had said nothing in the few days she had been in service at the Hall.

"Cat got your tongue, Miss Doris?" joked the housemaid.

"Yes, well no time to hang around. Esther, you have all the items you will need packed, the children's nightclothes and washbags?"

"Yes, Mrs Stanhope."

"And your things, they are with the luggage?"

"Yes, Mrs Stanhope."

"Excellent, then shall we make a start? Take the little one Esther, Doris you take my hand dear. Sally, we should return in a week or 2. Please ensure that the Hall is locked up securely when you leave." Sally did not like this new harsh side to the woman, she had taken on a somewhat cool air, it did not suit her.

"Mrs Stanhope." The coach pulled away taking the household onto the station. Sally remained on the step.

"Let us pray you will return with a lighter mood." Said the woman before returning to the dry of the empty hall.

Sally set about her tasks, singing to herself as she gave the rooms a thorough dusting. It was agreed that while the Mistress was away the house should be cleaned from top to bottom. Sally was to bring in some of the local girls to help for it would be too mammoth a task by herself. She was in the sitting room when the bell rang.

"About time and all." She muttered as she pulled open the door.

"Oh, Miss Mary, I do beg your pardon. I was expecting Flo and Lily from the village. 8 O'clock I told them, half past and no sign of the wretches. That's by the by, what can I do for you? You will have a cup with me?" Mary hesitated, not certain of the reception she would receive.

"Don't fret Miss Mary, her ladyships left early as she can this morning. Come in, don't get yourself wet out there." Mary was confused, she entered the Hall taking off her hat and cloak.

"Left, left for where Sally?"

"Did you not know, daresay you didn't things being what they are betwixt you both. She's gone off to stay with that cousin of yours, taken the children too, Esther an all." Mary was stunned, Sally could see this.

"And should the boy David return. What of that matter, what if David returns. Is he to find an empty house with his sister's gone. This simply won't do, Sally. It will not do one bit."

"Sit yourself down Miss Mary, no good you getting yourself all worked up. She is coming back, it's a trip is all, I'm sure of it. Maybe do the woman good to get away for a while, she's been couped up in here far too long these past weeks if you ask me. Tea?" Mary nodded, her mind still trying to make sense of why the woman would simply up and leave at a time such as this.

"Little one has stopped talking again, can't get a peep out of her since that day the Missus had her spat. Must be a mighty confusing time for the little lass."

"Oh, dear that is terrible to hear. What must the poor child be thinking?" Sally shrugged, things were going on here that even as an adult she did not understand so how was a young child meant to figure it out.

"If you ask me, there's something not right happening that we aren't made privy to."

"In what way do you mean Sally?" Sally poured the tea and sat down, her voice becoming a whisper in the already quiet house.

"I have seen that boy here, Tom, I saw him a fair few times but said nothing, not my business I says to myself. See him I did, him saying he wasn't here the night the little one was taken. Now, excuse me for being straight but you would think that his father being a policeman and all would have him up for answers, not so from what I hear. I like the Inspector, I do, but you have to admit there's something mighty strange going on here. Boy his age should be courting, turned down most the lasses in the village by all accounts. Spent many a time taking the youngster over to the farm, or so he says. Aint right is what I think."

"Sally! You cannot think that Tom has anything to do with this. My Robert has known the lad a long time, he is a sweet boy, yes, he has a shy nature but I won't hear of this nonsense. I am sure Inspector Billoughby has questioned him, it is not in his nature to overlook such a vital piece of information."

"Then answer me this, why did Grace get all uppity with me when I asked her about it?"

"Wouldn't you, if it were one of yours?"

"I may well do, I would make it my business to find the truth and that's all I'm saying."

Mary sipped her tea, she looked at the woman opposite with fresh eyes now. She would never have taken Sally to be a vindictive woman, perhaps she misjudged her?

"I must go, I have taken up far too much of your time Sally. Thank you for the tea and could you please inform me when Mrs Stanhope returns?"

"If she returns." Added Sally.

Robert shook his head, he felt angry that a person would have such wicked thoughts about a man as gentle and kind as Tom was.

"Bloody nerve of that woman. I spent many a year alone after my first wife died, I dread to think what she made of that! It means nothing, Mary, so the boy may have a schoolboy crush, he may invent reasons to go over there he doesn't want to share. So what! It hardly makes him a child snatcher or worse. I have a mind to march over there and put her straight so I do." Mary shushed her husband on hearing the door open behind him.

"Am I interrupting?"

"No lad, get yourself in here and have a bite to eat, rain isn't slowing any? Here, dry yourself off Tom." Tom caught the towel, as he dried his wet hair down he could feel an atmosphere.

"I can make myself busy if you are talking private things."

"Sit down lad, don't be daft." Mary passed a plate over to the young man.

"Tuck in while it's hot." Robert shook his head at Mary, he could sense she was to say something. Reluctantly Mary said nothing. The trio ate lunch, the talk was as light as the thoughts were dark.

"How was your morning Miss Mary, did you have a pleasant ride?"

"It was a wet ride, Tom. I called to see Mrs Stanhope, it appears she has taken herself and the children on a small trip to stay with my cousin. Still, the ride was pleasant enough." Mary, and Robert alike, could not fail to see the mortified look that spread over the young man's face on hearing this news. He tried to keep his voice steady, failing with each word that left his lips.

"When…why…is that wise…will she be back?"

"Leave a ruddy great house like that Tom, of course, she'll be back. How's that soup lad?"

"Why would she go without a word?" Mary stared at Robert, what was she to say?

"To me? I would think that was obvious as we had words, Tom, Why would she feel the need to inform me of a matter that is not my business." They both knew this was not what Tom meant.

"Right then, let's get back to work shall we?" Robert broke the painful silence.

"Yes, I too have things to do. I promised Cate I would stitch some cushions for the cottage."

Tom worked tirelessly that afternoon, his mind raging for his Elsbeth had gone without so much as a word. Why would she punish him so? Would she return? For how long was he expected to say nothing?

"Steady on there lad, you'll be digging to the other side of the world if you carry on at this rate. How on God's green have you managed to get so much done on your own?" Robert was standing staring out over the field that Tom had been digging over, expecting to see more that still needed doing than the narrow strip he was met with. Tom looked up, he too was shocked at his accomplishment.

"Was it the soup lad? I've often wondered if Miss Mary adds a secret ingredient to that soup, now I'm convinced of it." Tom laughed, he realised in doing so that he had not laughed for some time. The 2 men stood knee-deep in the mud as they laughed together at the impossible task Tom had completed in only an afternoon.

"I wager you broke a record of some description here lad, at the very least I am going to buy you a pint. Come on, enough for the day."

Molly and Albert Pratt stood behind the bar. They were deep in conversation as the farmers approached them.

"Aren't you a sight for sore eyes with your muddy boots and dripping wet hair? Get yourselves by that fire to dry off, a pint is it?" Trust Molly to always say the right thing.

"Thanks, Molly, evening Bert. Care to join us?" Molly nodded her permission to Albert, he had been short of the familiar male company over the past week, sure there had been customers but not any that Albert was happy to pass the time of day with. Albert placed the pints on the table, dragged out a chair and the trio talked about the weather, wives and the going's-on of the last week.

"I hear there's no news of the youngster?" They were bound to get to this topic, having covered everything of note thus far.

"Not a whiff of news I'm sorry to say. He's a bright lad too that one, he will turn up, mark my words." Offered Robert. Albert wasn't so sure.

"I hear tell that it's likely his Pa has claimed him back, rum sort from all accounts. He will have the lad thieving for him."

"Tom, here went with the Inspector to try to find him, isn't that right Tom?" Tom gulped his mouthful of ale, nodding his head in agreement.

"Scarpered by the time we got there of course. No telling where he might be now."

"Is it a fact young Tom that the pair are still over Brighton way?"

"Far as we know, the lad isn't with them, I expect they will hang around in case he comes back. Part of me hopes he does, leastways we will know where to find him." Robert nodded.

"Aye, they might be rum buggers but if he's with them Inspector stands more of a chance at finding the little one."

"Wouldn't fancy his chances on the streets alone in a strange place that's for certain." From across the room, Molly let out a squeal, the trio turned to see what the fuss was about.

"Well, as I live and breath! Get over here and give old Molly a hug." It was Connie, a very fancily dressed Connie at that.

"Hello, Mrs Pratt." Giggled the young lady as she wrapped her arms around the delighted woman.

"Look at you girl! I'm feared of wrinkling your pretty outfit. Where did you come from my girl? Tell me all your news. ALBERT, Albert get over here and mind the bar, Connie is here." Robert and Tom laughed at the grumbles muttered by Albert as he picked up the mugs and headed over to man the bar again.

Eight

Connie, it would seem, had come with news of her promotion in the company she had been working for. The position came with her own office and a staff of 4. The other news was that of her upcoming marriage. She playfully teased Tom about how he had missed a great opportunity in not fighting harder for her. Robert joined Albert at the bar.

"I'll daresay the youngsters will be happier without my company, eh, Bert?"

"Do we even understand half the things they talk about Robert? Motor cars, telecommunications, and such like. It's all a mystery to me and that's the truth. Good to see the girl doing so well all the same. Harsh life that one has had, she deserves some nice things."

Back at the table, Connie was regaling Tom with news of her job. She took to the work with ease, she explained, which terrified her on that first day.

"And now you're practically running the place, I'm that happy for you, Connie, I really and truly am. How will this affect your forthcoming marriage, will your future husband expect you to give it up?"

Connie smiled back at Tom, such a handsome face she thought, still, she had left this village behind and was content with her decision.

"It happens that my future husband is quite a modern thinker, we work at the same office and he is happy for me to continue to do so. He is a good man Tom, you would like him."

"Does this mystery man have a name?" The young woman looked embarrassed.

"Gracious, did I not say? Elliot, his name is Elliot." Tom grinned, the grin Connie remembered and loved.

"Sounds a grand name does that Connie or do we call you Constance?" She giggled.

"Tom Billoughby you are a one. Connie is good enough for us. How are your mother and father, oh, and Adam? I hear from Molly that

Adam and Cate have a home of their own now. It must be ever so exciting for them."

"One thing at a time. Ma and Pa are well, Adam, Cate and little Maisy are a day into their new home. I suppose you have heard of the going's-on with the young boy David?" Connie bit her lip, she had heard a few mutterings on her way through the village this afternoon, not least from Sally. It would be a shame to spoil this cosy reunion with her friend with tales of idle gossip. Gossip, that not for one minute did Connie believe.

"I have, it is a terrible thing to have happened. Let us speak of less upsetting things for the night, can we Tom?" Tom agreed, women were funny with talk of snatched children, maybe it was the mother instinct of wanting to protect all children that did it. Either way, they left the subject and moved on to talk of Daisy and her recent offer.

"Times are changing Tom, and for the better. Do you agree?"

"I say if a woman can do the same job as a man then why not, as long as it doesn't interfere with the raising of the children and meal times." Connie kicked the unsuspecting man under the table.

"Tom! You don't mean that?" Tom laughed, he still knew how to catch the girl out as well as he had when she wore braids and bruised knees. What a lifetime ago that seemed to him now.

"Of course I don't Connie. Take my Ma, she is a very clever woman, if she were a younger woman in today's world I am sure she could have a career in any area. Well done to you, I hope you go far."

The young couple talked well into the evening until eventually, Robert returned to the table.

"Ready to go young Tom?" Tom looked over at the clock on the wall, was it that time already?

"Connie, where are you staying tonight?"

Connie laughed.

"As you haven't been home you wouldn't know it, I am staying with you. I wrote to Grace some weeks ago and it was arranged."

"Now mind what I say, Tom, make sure you get some sleep, no talking into the small hours we have a busy day ahead of us. Connie, always good to see you, take care, my dear."

Saying farewell to Molly and Albert they made off for home. Tom felt pleasantly surprised that he got to spend some extra time with Connie, the girl that first stole his young heart. Any thoughts of Elsbeth had faded into the back of his mind for the time being.

"Oh it is good to see you, dear, come inside." Grace took the bag from Connie, placing it on the chair while she hugged the girl within an inch of her life.

"Just like old times." She said with an air of satisfaction.

"Thank you so much for letting me stay over the night Grace, I have missed you all."

"This is your second home dear, you will always be welcome here. Wait until Mr Billoughby gets home, he asks about you often."

"Where is Pa, he's out late tonight?"

"He had to go over to Canterbury, it sounds as though there may be news of young David. He should be back on the last train, Mr Nash is fetching him from the station."

Grace settled Connie into the now spare room where they talked of Connie's upcoming wedding. It wasn't long before the familiar call of Inspector Billoughby came from the kitchen.

"Hello there." Shaking off the rain from his hat he peered through to the parlour in time to see Grace and Connie appear from the back room.

"Bless my soul, I had quite forgotten you were coming today, come here and let me look at you." Connie flung her arms around the large man, she had missed this man that had stepped in as one of her substitute fathers.

"Will I do?" laughed the young woman.

"I would say you will more than do my dear girl."

"Have you news of David?" asked Grace as she readied a meal for her husband.

"Some, it would seem he may have been seen getting onto a small trawler in Brighton. The woman from the Obed Arms had asked around, which was ever so good of her, a drinker remembered seeing a child he had seen earlier on at the Inn climbing onto the boat as he strolled home along the dock. The woman called Joseph's telephone. Today we have been going over various listings of vessels that were moored, are they still there, where did they head to if they aren't that kind of thing. I have to say it is looking hopeful."

"Do you have reason to return to Brighton Father?" Billoughby shook his head.

"It may take a day or 2 but the information will be sent to me, this way I can try to catch up with any trawlers that have come our way, if that proves fruitless I may have to return."

"It's a start, more than we had a day ago." Added Grace.

"It is indeed, my love. Now, Connie, you must sit with me I would like to hear all your news." Connie pulled out a chair beside the Inspector and began retelling all the news of her upcoming promotion and wedding, in that order.

"Funny how things change." Remarked Billoughby as he listened to the girl's excited chatter.

"In what way dear?" Put in Grace. Billoughby stretched out, satisfied with his meal his body took on a more relaxed posture.

"I would have put money on these 2 getting wed, I would too! Now look at them, friends, I have no doubt. Our Connie all set for an important job, and a marriage. Tom, still farming and not a whiff of a romance, eh lad?" Tom felt uncomfortable at the question.

"Get away Mr Billoughby, Tom will find the right girl. Won't you Tom?"

"Trouble is Father, there are so many to choose from, taking my time you see." Laughed Tom. There was something about the forced smile thought Grace, still, she said nothing.

"Anyway, that's me off to bed. Some of us have to work in the morning." Tom bid them goodnight.

"Is Tom okay? He seems different."

"He is lass, changes you see, Tom was never one that took to so many changes all at once."

"Yes, I suppose. He seems sad, I can't explain it, just a feeling I get." Grace knew exactly what Connie was talking about. She too had noticed a sadness hovering over her son this past week.

"Nonsense, he's fine is our Tom. You women and your feelings." Laughed Billoughby.

"Now Connie, tell me to mind my own if you must. Who have you chosen to give you away?" Connie was stumped, she had not given this much consideration if she was honest with herself.

"I haven't. It never crossed my mind Mr Billoughby."

"I expect it would be Mr Farrow?" Offered Grace, not wanting to put the girl on the spot.

"Yes, quite right too. Thing is, I don't want you getting in a whirl about it is all I'm saying." Added Billoughby. Of course, he would be as proud as any man could be if she asked him, why wouldn't he? Mr Farrow and his wife did step in when the girl had no family, only right it should be him. Connie sighed, one of relief. This could have been tricky.

"Thank you Mr Billoughby for reminding me. I shall drop a note into the house on my way tomorrow. Sally tells me they have gone away for the week, shame really as I was hoping to surprise them with a visit."

"Yes, that would have been nice, they have missed you."

"And I, them."

"That's me done. Connie, I will see you in the morning before you head back. Sleep well."

Billoughby kissed Grace on the head as he made for his bed. It had been a long old day, pleasant for the most part he thought.

"I'll settle our guest in and be up in a minute dear."

Connie sat and stared around the room that was once hers. She missed the small village, not enough to return, not yet at any rate. She thought about Tom, was she doing the right thing? Sure that she was, for she loved Elliot, she settled down into the bed.

That night she dreamt she was a child again, running with the brothers in a gloriously yellow field of corn. She fell, Adam laughing at her clumsiness. Not Tom, always the hero he ran over to where she lay, held out his hand, and helped her up to her feet. The smile would have been visible to anybody watching the young woman sleep.

Tom was awake bright and early, as was his way. He quietly moved around the kitchen preparing himself a light breakfast and mug of tea. Sitting at the table he stirred the heated up porridge made by Grace the night before, she did make the best porridge he smiled to himself as he tucked into it. The door behind him creaked open.

"Morning Tom, still the early riser I see." Laughed a sleepy looking Connie.

"Hey you, why so early? I thought you would sleep in, this being your week off." Connie shook her head.

"It doesn't help me to sleep in, throws me for the rest of the week."

"Tea?"

"You carry on with that, it'll get cold. I can make my tea. Busy day for you?"

"This morning, yes. Not so much after lunch. What time is your train due?"

"Mid-morning, plenty of time yet. It has been good to see you, Tom, cleared up many a thought for me."

Tom was confused. What needed clearing up? It was she that had called off their short time together.

"What do you mean?"

Connie looked embarrassed now, when would she learn to leave well enough alone!

"That I had done the right thing, Tom. You and me, the trouble was, I thought of us more like brother and sister. Do you understand what I'm saying?"

Tom nodded, his face sullen as he looked at the young woman. Oh dear, I've upset him thought Connie. His face now changed into a large grin.

"I know what you mean silly. Didn't feel quite as it should, did it?"

"Oh, Tom Billoughby! You are a one, had me going there for a time. No, but the best of friends?"

Tom pulled Connie over to rest on his knee, his hug was that same old hug he would give her when they were younger.

"Always. Now, I have to get off to work, help yourself to porridge, just heat it through. Keep in touch my dearest friend." He was gone, leaving Connie standing alone in the kitchen.

Elsbeth woke early. The children slept quietly in the small cot beside her, she watched them for a long while as she lay in the early morning light. Occasionally Doris would cry out fearfully. What was going on in the child's mind? Why had she suddenly taken to silence again? All of these things perplexed Elsbeth, she had tried coaxing the girl into speech but to no avail. They had arrived late last night, her talk with Renton and his wife had been brief, hopefully, they could figure this out between them in the coming day's.

This wasn't the only reason for Elsbeth's visit. There was the matter of the children that Renton was hoping to place at the hall. He had written to Elsbeth and Mary regarding another 5 children that were in dire need of a warm home environment. They varied in age and if they were to escape the workhouse the adults would need to move fast.

Elsbeth felt it unimportant now to concern Mary with this new development, after all, why should she. She thought about Tom, how she had manipulated the situation with Esther to make it nigh on

impossible for him to continue any sort of relationship with the girl now that she had arranged for her to live under the same roof.
What had come over her? This moment of madness where the fear of losing Tom had become too much to bear. She knew that she had not felt love so deeply since her Wilf, she would not lose it a second time around, not to anyone.

"Morning Ma'am, Cook wants to know if you would like some tea?" It was that wretched girl, determined not only to try to take her Tom in actual reality but now from her thoughts.
"If I require tea, I will call for you."
Esther was taken aback by this reaction.
"Erm, yes Ma'am, sorry Ma'am." She fled to the safety of the kitchen where a more civilised conversation could be had.
Doris closed her eyes tight not wanting to be discovered awake by the angry woman.
"Doris dear?" whispered Elsbeth, thinking she had seen the child's eyes flicker awake.
There came no reply, maybe she imagined it.

By 8 they were all sitting around the dining table, the housemaids busily serving breakfast as the adults talked pleasantries. The children of the household sat at the other end of the table, trying to get a sentence from the strange visitor that couldn't speak. They were good children, of a calm nature with impeccable manners yet even they were feeling exasperated at the lack of response from the child.
"Dears, please do not frighten our little guest, she has had a long and tiring journey and will speak when she has rested."
Defeated, the children returned to their food at their Mother's request.

"It was so good of you to come, we have arranged to visit the children this afternoon if this meets with your approval? Our nanny will look after Doris and Dolly, the place we are going to is not at all suitable for the young one's." Continued Christine.
"It is most gracious of you my dear. I hope that won't be too much of a nuisance to your staff? I could have left the children at home, of course I could, I did not want any more upset or separation for them to have to deal with in light of their brother."

"Quite right, they pick up on so much."

"Which brings me to the other question." Renton lowered his voice somewhat as not to be heard by the children. "Is there any news of the young Master David?"

Shaking her head, Elsbeth swallowed a forkful of eggs.

"We are ever hopeful, we have the Inspector looking into every aspect of the disappearance. He is a good man, very thorough in his work and if anyone can track the boy down it is he."

Christine could not shake the feeling that the woman was somewhat cooler in her manner to the one they had met earlier in the year, maybe it was all too much for the poor dear she thought.

Breakfast over with the adults said goodbye to the children as the nanny marched them off to the nursery rooms. Elsbeth sat in the carriage next to Christine as they made for the place in the town where the meeting was to be.

"Do mind your step my dear, the ground is rather dirty with mud. Thank goodness we have rain at last."

They entered the building, it was damp yet brightly lit. Elsbeth looked around at the decaying old make-shift shelter. People of all ages huddled on cots, their faces, one after the other, with expressions of despair.

"It isn't perfect, but it's dry enough and they have regular meals which is more than can be said for some." Whispered Renton as they made their way through to the office at the back.

"Do they live here?" Enquired the shocked woman.

"They can stay for a week, we work it on a sort of rotation, gives everyone that needs it a chance. We can't do more than that at the moment."

Shaking her head, Elsbeth entered the office where they were greeted by a plump man, his face red and round.

"Good morning Renton, Christine. Do make yourselves at home. Madam, please sit."

Elsbeth took a chair as the man began to talk, he explained that the children in question were pleasant enough children, all orphaned and too young for the poor house, still younger for the workhouse and yet, that is where they would end up if a place could not be found for them.

"Is that something that happens often?" She asked.

"Far too often in my mind. Barely out of the womb and set to a life of hardship that no child should have to endure. They get stuck in the system and there's little they can do to escape it. We can keep them here a time, of course, it's no place for youngster's." Elsbeth nodded, the place was wretched.

"Can I meet them, are they here?"

"They are. If you wait I shall fetch them in."

The man made his way from the room.

"You know that you are under no obligation, Mrs Stanhope." Once again Elsbeth nodded.

Elsbeth thought hard in those next few minutes, 5 children would be a lot to take all in one go, still, she had managed thus far with 3. She would make it work.

Appearing at the door were 5 small and skinny faces, the dirt was smeared as though someone had tried unsuccessfully to clean it off. It was impossible to tell male from female as all had similar long shirts and short hair. They couldn't possibly all be boys, thought the woman as she stared at them.

"Come in children, don't look so worried. This is Mrs Stanhope. Mr and Mrs Stanhope you remember?" They nodded as they came further into the room. Mrs Stanhope has travelled a long way from the countryside to see you. Isn't that nice of her?"

Once again they nodded in unison.

"Hello children, You may call me Miss Elsbeth. Have you had something to eat this morning?" Elsbeth fished out a handkerchief from her bag, inside it was wrapped some flat sweet pastry.

"Would you like some?" They took it quickly, each one stuffing the whole piece into their mouth. Christine laughed.

"My you are all hungry ones."

The man turned his attention back to Elsbeth.

"2 boys and 3 girls, we can only guess at their ages I'm afraid. No more than 7 I would guess. We have Ruby, Martha, Lily, William and Jacob." They were a pitiful sight to behold and no mistake, in her mind Elsbeth had already decided what had to be done.

"Are you sure you don't want more time to think it over, Mrs Stanhope?"

The woman was resolute in her decision.

"No, thank you all the same. They can be ready to travel home within a few days?"

"They can. This is extremely generous of you Ma'am, you have no idea what it means to us, to them."

"It's the least I can do. We shall return the day after tomorrow. Good day Sir, goodbye children."

As was her word, Elsbeth returned 2 days later with Esther. They returned to Renton's home and with the help of Christine, they soon had all 5 of them looking clean and ready for travel.

"You have been most helpful, thank you so much for having us stay. I shall keep you updated with how the children are settling in, as I will should we have news of David. I will keep in mind your advice regarding Doris." Christine had tasked the kitchen boy with accompanying the group on their journey home.

"After all, they may be difficult to keep track of until you get to know them." She had insisted.

Esther and the young man kept the children more than occupied on the long train ride. There were the odd stares from other passengers along with comments that Elsbeth chose to ignore. Instead, she read a story to Doris. Doris was quite bemused at the number of children they were returning with. She clutched her teddy bear tightly for fear that one of these strangers would take a liking to him, with no David here to protect her. She succumbed to sleep, her tiny face resting against the seat as the train rattled on.

Nine

"When did they return?" Cate did not know what all the fuss was about.

"Yesterday, I told you. Does it matter?" Tom shook his head.

"Turned up with a whole heap of children, so she did."

"That's true brother, saw it with my own eyes. Must have a good 5 or 6 extra one's now. What is she planning on doing with them is my question. Will she adopt them as her own, or set them to work?"

Tom shrugged, did they not understand?

"Giving them a better chance is what, and why shouldn't she? There's not many that would stump up with an offer so generous mark my words!" He stormed out of his brother's cottage. What was it with some people that they could not see kindness?

"Well, that told us!" laughed Cate.

"Bit touchy there don't you think?"

"He's going through an awkward patch is all, give him space. Reckon it's come as a bit of a shock."

"What has?"

"Men! He's most likely still swallowing the loss of Connie."

"Ah, I see what you mean. Yes, he was rather taken with her and now she's getting wed. Poor old Tom, can't have been easy."

Tom walked around the edge of the gardens, he daren't approach the house, not with all that was being said about him.

"Hello, stranger. What brings you here?" It was Esther, was there no blasted escape from this girl!

"I'm not here, merely taking a shortcut. How was your trip?"

"So you have been keeping note of my whereabouts Tom Billoughby, I was beginning to think you were a lost cause to me." She laughed.

"Not at all, I have no reason to keep a note of where you are, I simply heard in the village that Mrs Stanhope had gone on a trip and taken the new maid with her." This was harsh and Tom knew it.

"I won't always be a maid Tom Billoughby, then who will be laughing!"

Esther marched off toward the hall, her ego not only bruised but crushed to a pulp.

"Was that the young Billoughby boy I saw?"

"Yes, Ma'am."

"What did he want?"

"I'm sure I have no idea, Ma'am. Said he was taking a shortcut, Ma'am."

"Good, I don't employ you to stand around the garden making small talk."

Blimey, what was the matter with everyone, thought Esther.

Billoughby poured over the lists that had been sent to him, Daisy had taken half and sat quietly in the chair opposite.

"Tea anyone?"

"That sounds lovely Mrs Billoughby, I'm parched."

"Dear, would you like some tea? You've been going over these for quite some time now." The Inspector looked up.

"Can't seem to make head nor tail of some of these. Tea would be nice thank you, my love. Daisy, how are you getting on with your half?" Daisy looked as confused as the Inspector.

"Mostly as well as you are by the sound of it."

"What we need, is a man that understands the sea and its charts. Back in a tick." Grace returned with a welcome tray of tea and scones.

"Where's he gone now?" She asked, bewildered at the sudden disappearance.

"I have no idea Mrs Billoughby. Said he'll be back in a tick."

True to his word the Inspector returned with someone behind him.

"Mr Nash, hello. Are we expecting you or, is this a social call?"

"Hello, Daisy love. The Inspector is in need of my brains, or so he claims. I knew they would be needed to solve a mystery someday." He chuckled.

"Little known fact, Mr Nash was once a sailor of sorts in his younger days."

"Were you really? I thought you had always been a grocer."

"I have, mostly. I rebelled a bit you see, didn't want to follow my Pa into the family business. Then I met the missus, hook, line and sinker as they say. Never went back to it but kept the knowledge."
"Lucky you did too, I can't make out these blasted charts."
Mr Nash took the papers from Daisy, sitting down he began to go over the scrawlings, stopping only to take a cup from Grace.

It was no time at all before the grocer had come up with a legible list of possibilities, neatly written on a large sheet of paper he explained the most probable course to the Inspector and Daisy.
"Ah, I see. It makes perfect sense when you think about it. Thank you so much, Mr Nash, this is a great help. By the look of things, they have been close by for a while. You think Hythe?"
"I do Inspector, it's the only possible stop from here." He pointed to the chart.
"You say the boats remain in the harbour a few days?"
Nash nodded as he sipped at his tea.
"It's what I would do, what most do. Takes awhile see, to unload the fish and pick up more supplies."
Billoughby scratched his chin.
"Hythe it is. If you could keep this to yourself I would be most grateful, don't want to get any hopes up until we have some solid news." Nash nodded in agreement.

The children were excited at the huge house. They had never been in a place so grand, or warm for that matter. Sally took them around the place, showing them where everything was, the kitchen was of particular interest to them. It smelt of cake and fresh bread, the large fire wafting the smell throughout the house and warming their cold little bones. Sally gave each a slice of hot buttered toast to take around on their small tour.
"These are the bedrooms. Girls will be in this one, boys, you are through that door down there. We will get to that soon enough. Well, what do you think, will you be comfortable here?" she laughed as their small faces lit up with delight and awe.
"You mean we are going to be staying in the house, Miss?"
"Well of course you are poppet, where on earth did you think. The stables?"
"Wouldn't be the first time Miss." The woman gulped, what these poor lambs have gone through was incomprehensible to her, she

wasn't a rich woman but she had always had a warm bed and food in her belly.

"I think we can say that you won't be sleeping in the cold anymore lovey."

Sally had wondered what possessed the Missus to invite waifs and strays into her home to begin with. They were dirty, riddled with lice and the like. Probably steal a few things here and there. Now, she stood and looked at them, Innocents they were, with nothing and nobody to care for them, it brought a tear to her eye and it was right then that she knew why Mrs Stanhope had opened her home. Yes, she was acting a little strange of late, but then who could blame her! One of her charges had been taken from right under her nose. Sally still wondered if Tom Billoughby had a hand in this with all his snooping around the place, there he was again! Lingering on the edge of the gardens.

"What did he want?" She asked Esther as the maid returned to help.

"Not me and that's for certain. Funny one he is and no mistake."

"Come along children, more to see and then lunch."

Elsbeth sat in the study, she could see Tom in the distance and her heart ached to run out to him. Foolish woman! She reprimanded her thoughts. There was a lot to keep her occupied with the latest group of children, not least the matter of seeking out clothing for them. They couldn't possibly continue in the items that they were wearing, kind as it was for Renton and Christine to donate them. No, they were to be part of the household therefore they needed to fit in as such. She rang the bell for Sally.

"Yes, Ma'am."

"Sally, we will need to purchase more clothing for the new children, I can't possibly put on the generosity of the locals again. They were so kind when our first arrivals came."

"Shall I speak to Grace, Ma'am?" Elsbeth shook her head.

"I don't think we shall, I hear there is a lady in Shadoxhurst that supplies various organisations, I shall give you the address and tomorrow you could take the buggy and measurements?" Sally was surprised that they wouldn't be calling on Grace, something was definitely going on.

"Yes, Ma'am. Anything else Ma'am?"

"No, that will be all for now." Leaving the room Sally couldn't help but wonder why this could not have waited, she shook her head at the way Elsbeth had become. Every inch the Lady of the Manor it would appear.

Billoughby coughed, it was a cough that people do before they are to say something important. Daisy looked over at the man, he had a concerned look about him as he watched the young woman. She smiled that smile.

"Out with it Inspector."

"Whatever do you mean girl?" His face now looked that of an embarrassed man.

"I can hear you thinking and it's getting louder!" She laughed.

Billoughby stood up and warmed his hands on the fire, it had started to get colder and his old bones could feel it. He shrugged, straight talk, that's what was needed here.

"Have you made a decision on your job offer?" There, he said it. Daisy gulped, how did he know? She had been careful not to mention it until the time was right.

"I haven't Sir. Who told you?"

Billoughby chuckled, she did not know him well enough.

"Nothing is sacred in this profession dear girl, neither should it be. Do you want to take the job?"

Daisy had thought long and hard about the offer, still, she was no closer to deciding than she was a week ago.

"I don't know. That's the truth of it, Inspector. I thought I did at first when Julian asked me. Now I am wondering if I am only considering it because of my feeling's for the man." Her pretty face flushed red, had she said more than she should?

Billoughby could well understand her conflicted thoughts, he too had been in a similar situation many years ago. He walked toward the door, putting his head around the frame and then closing it quietly.

"Daisy." He said quietly. "Do you recall why Grace and I moved here? We talked briefly about it, remember?"

Daisy nodded, not sure what this had to do with anything.

"I too was offered promotion in my younger day, had I taken it, I would now be sitting in the offices of the Superintendent. I had to make a choice you see, I chose Grace and my boy's. Not that I didn't think I could do the job, point is, I didn't want to do the job. I'm a policeman at heart, always have been, always will be. I solve problems, that's my nature. Would I have been a good Superintendent, yes I have no doubt. Would it have given me the wonderful family life I have now and the sense of achievement in my work, I don't think it would. You see, some of us do and some of us tell others what to do. Do you understand?"

"I think I do. Does Grace know this?"

"No, never felt the need to share a thing that I had decided on. I didn't ever want my Gracie thinking she held me back, because, and I mean this, she never did."

Daisy was stunned, more so that he had shared such a private thought with her.

"What you have to ask yourself, is what will make you happy? You can have both, you know that. If it is meant to be with this chap it will be, no matter your decision on the job. Now, you may think you are letting the women's movement down if you don't accept it, poppycock, there is as much valour in what you do now as there would be at the other place. Not as high profile mind you."

"I have written to extend my time to think on the matter. Thank you Inspector for your honesty. When I decide, you shall be the first to know. Now, back to work." She picked up the papers once again.

Tom walked along the lane, his mind in a constant whirl. What was he to do about this situation? He could no longer attend the hall, not now that girl was living there. Maybe, just maybe, a letter would be better. Yes, that was it, he would write his Elsbeth a letter. He doubted anyone would have access to the Mistresses private mail. But what would he write? He stopped to sit on the stone wall, his eyes looking over the fields that stretched before him. Would this always be the way of things? He thought about that last magical time they had spent together, the way the sun glimmered on her smooth silky black hair, how the feel of her smooth skin felt against his coarse rough hands, hands that even in his young age had been ravaged by hours of toil on the farm. Maybe she was too far out of his realm, maybe he had no business loving a woman of such a social standing not to mention the age difference. If people only knew that their love was good and true, they might stand a chance. For him, he would place an advert in the papers, he felt no shame in his love for Elsbeth. This wasn't the case for her and he knew it. She had responsibilities that might not withstand the backlash of a small community with its small-minded folk. He thought about the ticket he had securely hidden away in his box of special things. A new fresh start in another world, that might be the only answer. Yes, he would write that note, in it, he would offer up the suggestion of a new world far away from the stuffed shirts they called home. A smile spread across his face, standing from the wall he began to stride, this turned into a sprint as he raced home to put his thoughts to paper.

Tom could hear the raised voices from halfway down the lane as he approached the cottage. He could see someone standing at the front door, the figure dressed in black and perfectly still as though on guard. Nearing the gate he heard snippets of the conversation coming through the open door.

"Milton you must do something! This isn't right. You have no right to do this."

"Now Grace, please calm down, it is the procedure, you of all people know about procedure. It won't take long and we will have this whole misunderstanding cleared up."

"Procedure my eye! This is the word of one vindictive woman plain and simple."

As Tom slowed his steps he could see Daisy waving to him from the upstairs window. She looked frantic, her arms waving to him to keep walking. Tom caught the sentence like a thump to the ear.

"My boy would never do such a thing. We know who took the young lad, what do you think all of this paperwork is about? My boy would never hurt a child, nor anyone else for that matter." It was his father's voice. Lowering his head he walked straight past the gate toward the village. What the hell was going on?

Mr Nash pulled open his door.

"In here lad, hurry up about it. Bloody hell Tom, news is all around the village, I don't believe it for a second. Get in out of the way of prying eyes." Mr Nash practically pulled Tom off his feet in the rush to get him inside.

"What is happening?" Nash shook his head, a look of disbelief on his face.

"Damned if that interfering woman hasn't gone above your Pa and called in police from Canterbury. Have you been home?"

Tom shook his head.

"I was on my way there, walked right by at the insistence of Daisy. The things they were saying! You don't believe it do you, Mr Nash?"

Mr Nash did not, he had known the boys since they were born more or less, he was aware that you can never know a person fully, but this was ridiculous.

"No son, I do not, I have no doubt this is the doing's of another."

"What am I to do? I should go home and let them question me, I've nothing to hide. Does it not make me look guilty to be hold up in here?"

"Son, you need to gather your thoughts quietly, let them search the village, I'll tell them you went on an errand to Ashford for me. That will at least give you a minute to think, eh? Won't do your Ma and Pa any good to see you carted off in front of the whole village."

Tom gave in to Nash's idea, his parents were proud people. Before the sentence was cold came the loud knock at the door. Mr Nash pushed Tom into the pantry, he put his finger to his lip as he pulled on a coat.

"How do Gents, what can I do for you? Can we walk and talk, have to get back to the store, a busy time of day it is and my good lady will not thank me for leaving her too long, you know what women can be like, eh?" The laughter of the Policemen could be heard as the front door slammed shut.

Grace sobbed, in a way that her husband, nor Daisy had ever heard a woman sob. It was pitiful and painful to witness. It was not Grace's way, then she had never been faced with the prospect of losing a son to the gallows. It was not an exaggeration on her part, the threat was a very real one as well Billoughby knew.

"Come on, my love. It won't come to out, you know that don't you?" Grace could not be consoled, it was as though all those years of being the strong wife of a Policeman had caught up with her and the tears flowed fast and heavy.

"Got here as soon as we co… Oh, Ma, please don't take on so. Whatever it is, I'm sure we can sort it out." Adam put his arms around his mother, her head buried deep into his chest and her arms gripped around him in a way that felt she would crush the very life from her son.

"Where is Tom?" whispered Cate as she handed Maisy to her Grandfather.

"I spotted him from the window, told him to walk away." Added Daisy.

"Why? He's done nothing." Demanded Adam, Daisy stepped back quite startled at the tone of the usually friendly man.

"I thought it for the best, I didn't want him walking in on this." She waved her arm around the room. Billoughby nodded. He too felt this was the right course of action. Grace stared up at the pair, her eyes red and questioning.

"HE'S DONE NOTHING WRONG!"

"I know, my love. Won't do him any harm to have a while to gather his thoughts."

"WHAT THOUGHTS? GATHERING WHAT THOUGHTS, HE HAS NOTHING TO DO WITH ANY OF THIS." Grace continued to shout at her husband.

"Come along Ma, let's get you a drop of something to settle your nerves. Does us no good to be shouting at each other now, does it? Tom will come home when he needs to, I imagine he will take himself off to the police. He knows he's done nothing and so do we." Cate's tone was calm and even as she coaxed the woman into the kitchen.

"There now, sit yourself down and drink this." Handing Grace the mug of brandy, Cate shook her head to Adam as he tried to enter the kitchen.

"Leave it a minute will you darling?" Returning to the parlour Adam sunk into the armchair.

"Well, a right old mess and no mistake." He muttered.

"Grace love, how are you feeling now?" Grace patted the young woman's hand.

"It was all such a shock. One minute I was letting out Mr Nash, we were laughing about something I can't recall what it was now, I thought he had forgotten something and went back to open the door, there they were. Didn't ask to come in, just barged right through. Oh, Cate, he would never, you know that don't you? If I questioned him on his reasons for being there, his own mother, what chance does he have?" Cate held the woman's hand, her thumb stroking as she did so. It must have put all kinds of notions in the woman's head.

"I know Tom, as well as many, do I hope, this is simple, he was at the wrong place, at the wrong time is all. It will be straightened out once we find the boy, have faith in Mr Billoughby to find the answers." Grace looked at the kindly woman, a stranger to them not so long ago, yet now a part of the family as if she had always been.

"Thank you, dear, you are right of course you are. I am sorry for my hysterics, I could not bear to lose my boy to all of this."
Billoughby stood at the door listening, he could well imagine that Grace was feeling guilty for ever doubting Tom, this must be weighing heavily on her all-forgiving heart.

Back in the village, the officers had questioned just about everyone they could find. Some told of seeing Tom earlier in the day, others said nothing for he was thought of as a kind and honest chap amongst many. Eventually, the 2 men set off for the Inn. Molly was not at all happy about having them spend the night under her roof, not knowing why they were here at any rate!
"Looks mighty strange if we turn them away, love. Won't do the young fella any favours." She reluctantly nodded at her husband.
"I'll say this my love, better that no one starts running off their opinions in here tonight, they'll be shown the door." As was expected, the officers sat in the bar for the duration of the evening. Occasionally they would enter into conversation with the odd person. What was the village like, what were the Billoughby's like as a family? Needless to say, they got very short change from most. It was one thing to gossip amongst themselves, quite another to betray a friend. Albert smiled at Molly, he knew these people better than most and was happy in the knowledge that they didn't let him down.
"What can I get you, Robert?" Robert had come to see what was going on. He wasn't a nosey fella, Tom was his friend and employee. Albert quietly explained the situation, they were well out of earshot from anyone else. Robert shook his head and sighed.
"Lad wouldn't hurt a fly. Do we know where he is?" Albert did not, as he served Robert his drink one of the officers approached to which Albert winked at his friend.
"Evening, I don't think we've met as yet."
"Not to my recollection. And who might you be?"
"Sergeant Wainright, and you are?" Robert eyed the fellow up and down.
"A farmer." Wainright was little impressed with this man's manner. "Does the farmer have a name, Sir?"
"Aye. Be pretty daft if he didn't Sergeant. Still, I won't keep you. Albert, see you soon. Night Molly." Robert swiftly downed his ale,

his mug clattered loudly on the bar and he was gone, leaving the Sergeant standing dazed at the bar.

"Another Sir?" offered Albert, straining to contain the laughter that rose in his chest.

"That man. Who was he?" Molly stepped forward nudging Albert out of the way.

"That would be one of the farmers from here about's Sergeant, can't for the life of me recall his name, still, we get so many in here."

Mrs Nash took supper up to Tom, she had made up a cot in the back room upstairs. The room was used as storage mostly.

"You'll not be bothered by anyone this night." She had assured him with her kind smile.

Mr Nash had persuaded Tom to stay out of the way until the fuss had settled. On his rounds, he had called into the Inspectors for the second time that day to put their minds at rest.

"How is Gracie?" Billoughby thanked the grocer for his kindness as they spoke quietly at the door.

"You know, beside herself with worry. At least we know where he is and that he's safe. You are a friend indeed."

"Mind, you being of the force 'an all can't make it easy for either of you. I would never help a bad 'en Milton, you know me and you have my word on that. Lad's done nothing as far as I can see." Mr Nash left for home. He wouldn't be in the Inspectors shoes for all the gold in the world right now.

Billoughby watched his wife from the landing, she was exhausted by the days proceeding's and he felt it best to let her sleep. The brandy had helped with that. He would tell her in the morning of Tom.

The bell rang through the hallways in the big house. It startled the children as Elsbeth was getting them ready for their beds.

"That is a loud noise." Remarked one of the boys as she tucked him in.

"It is, now, do you have everything you need?" He nodded back to the woman.

"Good, sleep well. Goodnight children." She checked in on the girl's room on her way to the door, they were sound asleep. Who could it be at this time of the night? Esther had already gone to her room after sorting out the girl's and baby Dolly, Sally had left an hour ago as too had the other 2 housemaids. Elsbeth called out from behind the door.

"Who's there?" A muffled voice came back that she could not make out. Was it Mary? Opening the door she stepped back, it couldn't be.

"Are you going to keep us on the step dear?"

"Mother! What on earth brings you over this way at this time of the night. Hello father, come in, come in." They were a sight for sore eyes and no mistake. It had been too long.

"Did you not get our message dearest? We sent word that we were planning to visit." Elsbeth looked over toward her visible desk in the study and its ever-growing pile of letters.

"I've been away, scarcely back a few day's and not a moment to myself to catch up with correspondence. Oh, it is so good to see you! Have you eaten, you must be starved!"

They pulled in their cases, much to the bemusement of their daughter.

"Please, let me help you with that. Are you staying a while?"

"A couple of weeks if that works for you dear." Huffed her Father as he lifted the last of the luggage from the cart.

"I'm so sorry, I sent the stablehand home as I didn't require him again tonight. Sit yourselves by the fire and I shall take care of the horse." Disappearing through the courtyard, Elsbeth quickly saw to the tired old horse. She fed and watered the beast, then tossed a warm blanket over his back.

"That should do until the morning old fella." She patted his head affectionately before returning to the house.

"We can eat in here." She announced as the smell of hot stew filled the air.

"You're going to join us, dear?"

"I thought I might, I haven't had time to sit and eat today. The children have kept me far busier than I imagined today. Father, help yourself to bread and wine." As they ate Elsbeth's parent's caught their daughter up with all of their news.

"It seems an age since we last saw you, dear. That is why your father and I decided we would come to stay, I do hope it won't put you out at all but we have missed you so." Elsbeth could not have been more pleased for she had missed them too. Her face reflected the happiness their arrival had invoked on her.

"Now, you must tell us all about the children. We think it's wonderful that you have opened your home to them. Tell me, dear, whatever made you think up such an idea?" Elsbeth looked down into her bowl, her face becoming sad in its expression.

"It was the right thing to do mother. I have long wanted children of my own, a wish that could never be granted as we know. Is it selfish that I partly do this for my own needs?"

Father looked across at Mother, his soft eyes showing the smallest of a tear waiting to fall.

This daughter, was an angel and saviour if ever there was a person on earth that could claim this divine title.

"You are not selfish my dear, never have been and never will be. That you feel gratification from this act is not such a bad thing is it? Many say there is no such thing as an unselfish act, but do them we should." Her Father was bursting with pride at the accomplishments of his daughter and it showed. They both realised the struggle Elsbeth had gone through with Wilf and then Stanton, not to mention the yearning she carried for children of her own.

"You have done well my girl, let nobody tell you otherwise." Added Mother.

"Will we see Mary? I do hope so. I know you always speak so fondly of her in your letters, we're just dying to meet her." Elsbeth felt herself straighten up at the mention of her sister-in-law. How would she explain her unwarranted outburst to the woman, for she had come to realise that she was so very wrong in her chastisement of the person she had come to think of as a sister.

"Mary and I have quarrelled, it was of my doing I'm ashamed to say."

"Oh, my dear we all have our off days, the thing to do is set it right, isn't it?"

"I'm not sure how to Mother." The sadness and despair were noted by both parents.

"We shall get to that. I assume there is no news on young David?" Elsbeth shook her head.

"I just wish he would come home. He was a bright star, is a bright star! He could light up the room with that cheeky boyish innocence, he is missed more than you can imagine. The longer he's away, the harder it becomes for me to think I will ever have him back." The tears flowed from the distraught woman's eyes. She had held it together for what seemed an age, now, in the presence of the people she knew and loved best, they could not be contained. Her mother rushed to her side, comforting arms that seemed to make Elsbeth feel shielded from harm wrapped around her now. These were the arms that told her everything would be okay.

"There, there my dear. We will find him, we will bring him home where he belongs. Seems to me you need a decent night's sleep my girl. I will bring you breakfast in the morning, you are not to leave your room until I say so, Mother always knows best. Father and I can spend some time getting to know our new extended family."

"I'm quite looking forward to meeting the brood. Now, point us in the right direction and we'll all get some sleep. Mind what your mother says dear, sleep in and enjoy the rest." Elsbeth nodded, she welcomed her parent's take-charge attitude, no if's or but's were just what she needed to hear.

Alone in the sitting room, Mary waited for news from Robert. She stroked the 3 faithful dog's that lay at her feet absent-mindedly. It wasn't long before she heard the door in the kitchen close.

"Is that you dear?"

"It is my love. Sorry I have taken a little longer than I said."

"Did you discover what is happening?" Robert slumped into the seat beside her.

"Police down from Canterbury." Mary sat bolt upright in the seat.

"Have they found David?" He shook his head.

"Sadly no, they are here at the request of a certain busy-body from the village, that someone feels Inspector Billoughby is harbouring a criminal in the form of his own son. Can you believe such nonsense! I ask you, there are some that have too much time on their hands." Mary was shocked. Why would anybody accuse the young man?

"Have they arrested Tom?"

"Nope, they would have to find him first, which they haven't. He hasn't run off, just settling somewhere quiet to gather his thoughts." Mary did not like the turn this whole situation was taking.

"We must find David, it's the only thing that will save the lad."

"Inspector is heading off tomorrow, he has reason to believe the little fella is travelling with fishermen, having escaped the clutches of his so-called father. From what I hear, the 2 men that took him were apprehended on their return to Canterbury. Made out they had never stepped foot in this part of the world. No proof to say they had so they were let go. You can see how that puts young Tom in the noose"

"But they had witnesses to say they were seen with the boy."

"Ay, they did that. Can't be bothered, that's their problem. If they went to Brighton and spoke with the lass they would know this. They won't as far as I can make out, wasting time they reckon as they have a suspect right here on their doorstep." Mary was appalled.

"Can't we do something?"

"I'm not rightly sure we can, my love. Grace in a right state 'an all, so I hear."

"Oh, Robert, this is all so very disturbing. I've a mind to go to Brighton myself and bring the woman back, that she can tell these officers exactly what she saw." Robert jumped up.

"You mean that Mary?"

"Yes, I mean that."

"Right you are, first thing tomorrow I'll set you on a train, take Billy with you. I'll give you money, she might need some persuading, bring the woman here if you can. I would go with you but I'm short my best farmhand as it goes."

"Oh, you are the best husband."

True to his word, Robert waved Mary and Billy off that very next morning. He hoped against hope that her trip would bring back the proof that was needed to clear Tom's name.

Ten

David was excited at the prospect of going to a place he knew. He lay in his makeshift cot below deck and dreamt that amongst the crowds in the marketplace he would spot Miss Mary or Miss Elsbeth. He knew full well that the men that took him had made threats, threats that even as a young boy such as he was, he took very seriously indeed. Still, Freddie and his men were more in number and stronger too. They had muscles the size of rocks, not at all like the 2 men, they were flabby and drunkards. He could tell they weren't fit men by the whistling sounds they had made when they walked. No, Freddie would be more than a match for them if they were to meet again.

"' Ere, nipper, time to wake. We're coming into harbour soon enough." Freddie shook the foot that was sticking out of the blanket.

"You good lad?" He stretched out his arms and pushed back the covering.

"I'm good Captain." He yawned.

"Good, breakfast ashore today, my treat." It was light when David went topside of the trawler. The sky was cloudy, small pockets of blue pushed their way through.

"Feel that chill lad? Winter's on its way."

Freddie had pondered what they were to do with the lad through the winter months, he knew a boat at sea was no place for a youngster in the harsh conditions that the season brought with it. Secretly he was hoping that they might gain a clue or 2 from the stopover in Hythe. Not that he wanted to be rid of the child, the truth of it was, he had grown quite fond of the lad, as too had the crew.

"Recognise anything?" David looked across the shoreline. He had spent the day here, that was true because he recognised the name, nothing looked overly familiar as yet.

"Not from here Captain Freddie." Freddie grinned.

"All looks much of a muchness I daresay from this angle."

They secured the trawler on the sand, logs were set underneath to roll it over the shingle. They planned to have a few days ashore, Freddie knew that these men had their needs and would not be content to put up with a few hours, they would be in no fit state to leave that day. Not that he blamed them, mind. He too once had that urge, not so much since his one true love had gone. He had been a jack the lad, some might have said, a girl in every harbour if not 2! Then he met her, the woman that was to steal his heart and ruin him for all the looser women he had known. He shrugged, no point going down that road.

"Ready lad?" Was he ever! David was filled with a mixture of excited expectations and worry. He loved life aboard the trawler, the prospect of being discovered would bring an end to this, he missed his sister's that was true. He knew they were in the safest hands with Miss Elsbeth and Miss Mary. He missed the lambs, the piglets, yes, he missed the piglets most of all. They had funny little snouts, not at all as smelly as people would have you think. He missed Mr Robert and Tom, they treated him like a grown-up, said he could make a proper farmer one day.

The marketplace was packed with people, even for that early time of the day. David sniffed up, such wonderful smells drifted on the breeze.

"Spices lad, that's what you can smell. Beats the small of cold fish wouldn't you say." Laughed Freddie as they weaved through the crowded street.

"Ain't so bad Captain, smelly fish I mean. Ain't so bad at all."

"Stick close by me lad, don't want you getting lost again now do we?"

David clutched the man's hand tightly, he absolutely did not want to get lost again! The crew had gone their separate ways leaving David and Freddie to their own devices. They sought out a place to eat, savouring the hot fresh bread and the steaming porridge flavoured with fresh honey.

"Tasty?"

"It's great, I never tasted porridge like this before and Miss Mary made some lovely porridge." There was that name again, Freddie did not raise questions of the names that slipped from the young child's lips. The last thing he wanted was to put the boy on guard about what he said. After breakfast they walked leisurely around the marketplace, Freddie pointing out different wares that came from foreign lands, silks and spices, fruits and crafts.

"Do you fancy travelling to other lands young David?" David had never thought about such a thing, the land he lived on seemed big enough.

"Would it take very long Freddie?"

"I imagine it would. Not like the travels we have, few days here and there. I imagine it would take months." David screwed his nose up.

"I don't think I like the idea of that one bit." Freddie ruffled the child's hair affectionately.

"Me either son, me either."

Reverend Moore ran his hand across the soft fabric, he had never felt cloth as soft as this.

"Silk you say?"

"Pure as they make it Sir."

"Exquisite, simply exquisite."

"Someone special Sir? The scarf, is it for someone special?" Reverend Moore blushed.

"Not in the way you might think my dear woman. A dear friend, the colour captures her eyes beautifully, Yes, I shall take it, oh, and this too." The Reverend picked up a similar scarf in vibrant blue.

"Yes, these will do wonderfully." Paying the woman he tucked the package into his bag and carried on through the crowded street.

"Did you find anything you liked Reverend?"

"I did indeed, Inspector. How are you managing, spotted anyone yet?" Billoughby glanced around the busy road.

"Nothing as yet, Reverend. Still, the trawler is definitely sat out on the shingle, they must be around here somewhere. I pray it isn't a wasted journey, what with all that is going on at home I could have done without this today of all days. Remember, keep your eyes peeled Reverend." Tobias nodded, they were not here today merely for the market, although he felt it made a pleasant change. No, today they were here on a mission, a mission to find the child. It was all very exciting for the Reverend, true to say it was a very serious situation, all the same exciting to the man of God.

"Meet up at 11 near the tavern, I'll go this way, you take that side," Billoughby suggested as he headed off across the road.
"You can count on me, Inspector."

Billoughby searched up and down the streets for what seemed an age, looking at his pocket watch he noticed it was time to get to the tavern, the Reverend was most likely there waiting. He had passed the sweet stand many times through the morning, not stopping as Grace's words echoed in his ears.
"We need you fit and well husband, you really must try to contain your sweet tooth!" He smiled as he recalled the conversation not more than a week since. Bless her sweet heart trying to keep his impending middle from expanding. One wouldn't hurt, surely? He browsed the selection.
"Anything take your fancy dear?" Encouraged the plump lady. He knew, truth be told, that most of what lay before him took his fancy!
"The good lady wife has warned me off, I'm considering which will do me the least harm." He laughed.

"Come on lad, time for a treat as promised. This way." David was looking forward to his treat. Freddie had told him of all the wonderful new sweet treats that the marketplace had to offer. They wandered over to the stall, David rubbed his hands when he saw the mixture of toffee's that had been spread out on the lace tablecloth, there was so much to choose from. He couldn't take his eyes off them. Freddie was busy passing the time with another fella that could not decide what he wanted either. Eventually, David decided on what he would have.
"Captain Freddie, can I have one of those?" He pointed to a huge Lollipop, its colours swirled between each other making it look like a rainbow. David was captivated, not least because as good as it was to look at, he could eat it into the bargain and that couldn't be a bad thing! Freddie turned to see the choice the young boy had made.
"That's almost as big as your head, lad."
The man behind Freddie drew closer, he crouched down as he stared at the child.
"What are you doing Mister? Leave the lad alone, eh." Freddie didn't like the way this fella was looking at David. Still, the man didn't budge.
"David?"

Freddie gently pulled the boy behind him.

"What business is this child to you?" Demanded the Fisherman. Billoughby stood up.

"Oh, Inspector! Well done you, my word I was beginning to think we were on a fool's errand." Billoughby nodded to the Reverend.

"Inspector? You're a Policeman?" Freddie was confused. David stayed hidden behind his coattails.

"Come forward, son, you're not in any bother."

David stepped out from behind his new guardian, still clutching the Lollipop in his hand.

"Excuse me Gents, is anyone going to pay for that?"

Reaching into his pocket the Reverend paid the woman, not taking his eyes off the boy.

"Come with us, we were going for a bite at the Tavern and I'll explain." Replied Billoughby to the Fisherman.

"How do I know you're not these fella's that snatched the lad?" Persisted Freddie, for he was not about to hand the boy over to just anyone.

Billoughby pulled out his badge.

"Is that proof enough for you? David, son, tell the man who we are will you?"

"They said they would hurt the Missus, and my sisters, Mr Billoughby. They said if I didn't do what they said they would go back and hurt Miss Mary and, well, everyone. I didn't want to steal nothing, Mr Billoughby. Then I run away, see. I hid in the boat and Captain Freddie found me. He ain't done nothing wrong, Mr Billoughby, honest he ain't. Just gave me food and bed is all."

Billoughby pulled the child from the ground into a bear hug. He was so happy to see him, Tom would be saved now, surely.

"We have missed you, you little scamp." Freddie bowed his head, he didn't quite know what to say.

"Come, let's eat and we can straighten this whole thing out."

Freddie followed the men to the Tavern. Once the food and drink had arrived and they had started to relax, Freddie gave his version of the events.

"If I'd known any of this I would have brought the nipper straight back. I thought he was alone in the world, Inspector, couldn't bear for him to be left to the streets so I let him stay on board. He's a good little fella, aren't you? Didn't shirk from any work neither. Was like having a boy of my own, so it was. David, why didn't you tell me? Old Freddie would have seen you right." David's expression saddened.

"I liked being a Fisherman, Captain Freddie. If I told you, you would have taken me back, then they would have done for Miss Mary and the Missus, they said."

"Oh, son. You know I wouldn't have let them. Me, and the crew would have seen them off."

Tobias could not stop smiling.

"Everyone is going to be so pleased to see you." He stammered as he swallowed down another piece of steak pie.

"Are you in the area for a while?" Asked the Inspector.

"A few day's, then we are set for Whitstable."

"Would it be an imposition to ask you to make a small journey with us to David's home, I am quite sure Mrs Stanhope would like to thank you in person."

Freddie was now realising that his time with the pleasant child was drawing to a close. His heart was heavy, for he had quite taken to the child.

"Please." Continued Billoughby.

"She has been out of her mind with the worry of it all, I am certain she would like to hear from you that David's ordeal was not altogether as dreadful as she has been imagining."

Freddie reluctantly nodded in agreement, if it had been his child, he too would wish to thank the rescuer in person.

"I'll have to track one of my lads down and let them know."

"Of course. We shall remain here for your return."

Mary left the Obed Arms, she felt it had been a wasted journey and was angry at herself for thinking that she could make a difference for poor Tom.

"Home again." She said quietly to her companion.

"No luck Miss Mary?"

"No, the woman has family troubles in Portsmouth and they have no idea when she will return."

"What do you think is going to happen to Tom?"

"I dread to think, without the woman, or the child, it does not look good for him."

The journey home was a quiet one. Mary lost in thoughts of what she knew could well happen to Tom and her companion, asleep for the most part. Robert was waiting as they stepped out of the station. He could see the look on his wife's face meant that they had not had the success she was hoping for.

"Never mind, my love. Something will come from all of this, Tom will be okay, you'll see." His strong arms embraced her, much to the embarrassment of the young travelling companion.

"What's the matter with you lad, a man can't hug his wife?" They boarded the cart and set off on their long journey home.

Sally positively screamed through the large house.

"MRS STANHOPE, MRS STANHOPE, COME QUICK. OH, DO HURRY UP. MRS STANHOPE!" Elsbeth came running down the stairs.

"Whatever is the matter woman that you need to bellow like a…" The sight of David standing in the hall was too much for Elsbeth. The room span as her legs gave way.

In the parlour, Elsbeth's mother held her hand. As her eyes opened she knew she hadn't imagined it.

"Oh, my dearest boy, my dearest child. Where have you been? I have missed you so very much. Your sisters, Sally fetch Doris and the little one. Come here, let me look at you, it is you, it is you." Grabbing David she pulled him close to her. She smelt as pretty and fresh as ever, thought the child as he rested his head on her shoulder. Billoughby sat in the kitchen with Elsbeth's father. They talked about the enormous strain that Elsbeth had been under. Her father explained that Elsbeth had told them all about the anger she had unleashed on Mary and Grace.

"She didn't mean it you know, not her nature. She has been that upset with this whole bloody incident, not knowing who to turn to. You must tell your wife that she is so sorry for what she said and how she behaved." Billoughby nodded, he knew this to be true.

Back in the parlour, David was introducing Captain Freddie to Mrs Stanhope.

"I don't know how I can ever repay your kindness, Sir. I thought he was lost to us forever and yet, here he stands, all down to your kindness and generosity." Freddie grinned, my, but she was a handsome woman, something about her that he could not quite put his finger on.

"It was my pleasure Ma'am, he is a charming young lad. I'll not lie, I shall miss his company and that's the truth. We had quite an adventure there for a time, didn't we nipper?" David agreed, he too would miss the Captain.

"You must come back and visit, as often as you are in the area. I insist."

Freddie refused to take a reward of any sort from Elsbeth.

"Promise me, if he ever needs anything, you too for that matter, you will leave word at the places I have written. I might not get here straight off mind, but I give you my word I will get here."

Tom sat back against the hedge. It had taken him most of the day to leave the Nash home, he did not want to be spotted by anyone thus getting them into any trouble. From where he was sitting he could see the Hall clearly, he ducked down as the large door opened. What was this? He stared on in disbelief as he watched his Elsbeth embrace the tall, handsome man. The man kissed her cheek. That was all he needed to see. Scrambling from the ground he bolted back into the cover of the trees. His mind was racing, where would he go? One thing was for certain, she had forgotten him.

The cottage looked still, tip-toeing through the back door and into the kitchen, Tom listened for any sign of occupants. There were none. Grace and Cate had gone to Cate's home for the afternoon. Tom quickly made for his room, once there he threw various items of clothing and money into his sack. Reaching under the floorboard to his secret place, he fished out the box. He checked inside, good, it was still there. Tucking the box carefully under the clothes he stared around the room he had slept in for all of his life. It would be sad to leave, he knew this, but go he would have to or risk the hangman's noose. He was not going to wait around for that to happen! One last check and he closed the door behind him.

Downstairs he considered leaving his Ma and Pa a note, no, that would surely land them into some kind of trouble. He ducked back out and off away into the fading sunlight.

Elsbeth called the Inspector to one side, she had to find out what was happening with Tom. It had been so long since they had seen each other.

"Yes my dear, what can I help you with?" The woman shuffled her feet awkwardly, how was she going to word this and not raise suspicion?

"I wondered how the family were doing, I will of course call by to give my apologies to Grace." Billoughby laughed.

"Mrs Stanhope, I am sure my Gracie will understand your outburst given that she too is a mother, her reaction would well have been the same as yours. There is no need of apology my dear."

"I feel I must. How are the boys?" Billoughby sensed her uneasiness.

"They are quite well, thank you. Now that the youngster is home safe and sound there will be an end to this foolish gossip concerning Tom. It has had us all quite worried I can tell you. A word of warning, if you don't mind me speaking out of turn, keep on your guard around Sally, she has a nose for gossip as we have found to our cost."

"In what way, Inspector?"

"That she was the person that called in the police from Canterbury, thought I wasn't carrying out my duties where my son was concerned." Elsbeth was shocked, that this woman who worked under her roof could potentially have brought a noose around Tom's neck with her idle chatter and mean mindedness.

"I shall certainly keep that in mind, thank you for bringing it to my attention, Inspector. What a wicked thing to think of Tom, he would never hurt a thing!"

"A visit to dear Mary would not go amiss either if you don't mind me saying?" Elsbeth nodded, she had intended to see her sister-in-law and clear up this mess.

"Duly noted, Inspector. She will be so pleased that we have David home safe, we are so much in your debt." Billoughby was pleased with the outcome, the boy had been gone for far too long. He bid them farewell, eager to get home and give the news to Grace and the rest of the family.

Grace could sense that someone had been in. She looked around to see if anything was out of place, no, everything as it should be. Then why did she get this strange feeling?

Her thoughts were interrupted at the arrival of Billoughby.

"Hello in there, it's only me." He placed his hat and coat on the hook in the hallway.

"Hello dear, I've only stepped through the door now myself. How was your trip? Did you have any luck?" Billoughby swept his wife up in his arms, his smile told her he had.

"You didn't find him? You did! Oh, Milton, that is the best news, where was he, how is he? Is he alright? Not hurt or anything?"

"Woman, pause for breath! One thing at a time. We did find the little fella, fortunate we were too I should think. He is fine, not hurt at all and happy to be home. Our young David has been living the life of a sailor, a chap named Freddie rescued the lad in Brighton, took to him he did. Thought the lad had no one so kept him with his crew. I have to say, he had a sadness when he had to leave the lad, proper kind soul he was." Grace smiled, she was so pleased with the news.

"And Tom, where is Tom?"

"Is he not back here?"

"No, not seen sight nor sound of him since yesterday, I thought you might have tracked him down on your way back."

"No, I called at the grocer's, Nash said that he had made up the bed and left, he thought he had come home."

Grace could feel her stomach knot, pulling away from her husband she ran for the stairs.

"Grace, Gracie love. What's the matter?"

She pulled the cupboard door open, a few old work trousers and a shirt were all that was left hanging in there. Sitting on the edge of the bed she looked around the room.

"Oh, Tom." She whispered.

Tom did not stop walking, it was dark now and the air was turning chilly. He had no idea where he was going, all he knew was that he couldn't stay. Not now.

Eleven

The job was a simple one, at any rate, it would tide him over for now. The town of Deal wasn't such a bad place and he got to sit by the sea of an evening. Mostly he kept the cellar tidy and cleared away plates and glasses. He got a bed for the night and a few pennies to buy food. He had money, of course, it was one thing he made sure of when he had left, still, he wanted to save that if he was to start a new life in a few months. The Landlord tried engaging him in conversation, which Tom kept to a minimum. They had no complaints about his work, he was strong and he got the jobs done. Occasionally he would join them for a drink after they closed up for the night, they were a nice enough lot. He planned to stay awhile and move on again when the time was right, not something he shared with his employers. It had been a month since he had left the countryside he called home, another month and it would be Christmas. How the time had flown by.

He often thought about his family, he wondered if they were coming to terms with his leaving. They must have realised by now that he had no other choice. He thought about young David, hoping that wherever he was he was okay. Baby Maisy would be growing fast, it would be her first Christmas and he was sure that Adam and Cate would spoil her rotten, and why not.

"Penny for them." Interrupted the Landlord.

"They're not worth your money." Laughed Tom. He knew this was a lie as the words left his mouth.

"It will start to get a might busier, you up for that in the coming months, Stan?" Tom nodded. It would take him a good while to get used to the name, he felt it best to change his name in case anyone came asking questions.

"I am, a bit of hard work never hurt anyone." Was his reply.

"Good lad, that's what we like to hear. I say we've had some right one's here over the years. Big an all but no stamina you see. Spoonfed on honey if you ask me, not you, Eh, Stan?"

"No, worker all my life and that won't change any." The man patted him on the shoulder.

"Night lad."

"Goodnight Sir."

"It's been over a month now Milton, we've heard nothing. Why wouldn't he let us know he is safe?" Milton scratched his head, he had been asking himself the same question for weeks.

"The way I see it, my love, he doesn't know the lad was found. As far as he's concerned he's still wanted. My thinking is that Tom feels it better to stay away for our sakes."

Grace knew in her heart that this was likely the case, but she wanted her boy home. Yes, one day he would marry and leave the nest, she was prepared for that day. Not like this, this was unbearable. Mrs Stanhope had called by every day to be told the same thing, no news. Good of her, thought Grace, but then she too had suffered the loss of the child David for a while, she too knew the anguish. Grace had busied herself helping out with the new children, taking on the role of seamstress once again to clothe the poor mites. The woman had made her peace with Grace, Mary had been a little harder to convince, but it had worked out in the end.

"Adam said he will be calling later, so good of him to have taken Tom's place at the farm. I know Robert would have struggled without him." Billoughby added.

"Yes, hard workers both, the wage will come in handy for them too especially now they have the cottage and little Maisy. Still, I do wish Tom would send word."

Elsbeth gathered the children in the newly painted schoolroom. She was to teach them herself, helped by the Reverend Moore they would begin to tackle reading and writing. The children had settled into the house incredibly well, sure there had been a few hiccups in the first month, nothing they could not deal with. Cate had been coming over every Thursday afternoon to play the piano and teach singing, this is where they came to discover that one of the children, Ruby a child of 7, had a particular gift with the keys.

"It's amazing." She had said to Elsbeth and the Reverend.

"I have never known anyone pick it up as quickly and proficiently as she has." Reverend Moore was delighted at the child's ability. He wondered if Cate should give her extra lessons alone.

"It's certainly an idea, Reverend, although I expect it would seem that we were not giving the other children a chance if we did that. I imagine it best to keep them all in their group until we find each child's talent." Elsbeth had never been one to single out children, she felt they should all feel special. Tobias nodded, he could understand the woman's aims.

David was pleased that there were 2 new boys for him to take under his wing. William and Jacob followed him everywhere, Jacob was the elder of the trio and yet he hung on every word that came from David's lips. William was the quieter of the boy's, he much preferred books to mud and animals. He was often found in the library, and though he could not yet read all of the words he would sit and look at them for long periods of time.

Martha and Lily were inseparable, it was thought they may be sisters, but there was little evidence to support this. They adored baby Dolly, often walking her around the gardens in her pram. Ruby didn't often spend time with the 2 girl's, they would invite her, they liked the child very much but she would always decline in her quiet voice. Ruby watched Doris, it had not gone unnoticed that Doris didn't speak. The other children thought she couldn't so paid no mind to it, David couldn't understand why his sister had taken to silence again.

"Why has she stopped Miss Elsbeth?" He would ask. Elsbeth simply shook her head in despair, she had no idea either. Elsbeth had hoped that Doris would begin to speak again on David's return but she didn't.

"She will, in time my dear." Even the Inspector failed in his attempt to coax the child this time. It seemed that Doris was happy in her silence, wandering around the big house, ever clutching her ragged bear.

Mary stood in the hall, she gazed around as she often did, the memories swaying around like ghosts flying at a great height. She had come to instruct the children in math. David rushed over, flinging his arms around her skirts. She smiled, so fond of this boy that she was.

"You won't be as loving when you find out what I'm here for!" She laughed, for she knew that the little chap had no interest in numbers. Standing back from her David placed his hands on his hips. Mary waited for the obligatory 'I hate math' it didn't come, instead,

"Captain Freddie, says I should like math, if I'm to be a fisherman and stars, he said a good fisherman should know his stars." Well, this was a turnaround, thought Mary.

"He is right, a good fisherman knows his numbers and the skies. I must say, young man, I have never heard a sentence that has pleased me as much."

"Captain Freddie is a great fisherman, one day Miss Mary, I will be a great fisherman too."

"I have every faith that you will my boy. Now, can you gather up the children for me, if you can tell me how many we have in class today I may take you to see our newborn lamb."

David ran off to find the children, they were in various parts of the house and garden, bemused when he asked them to line up so he could count them, but compliant.

"7 Miss Mary, including me." He shouted triumphantly. The woman laughed, she had wondered if he would add himself, clever boy.

"Come along children, take a seat and we shall get started." The children took their seats in the small cosy room. It had been Elsbeth's wishes that the room was not oppressive and the decorators had done a wonderful, bright job of it. Mary stood at the chalkboard, she was scribbling down numbers.

"First things first. Good morning children." The room echoed as the children bid her a good morning, Doris merely waved her teddy.

"Today, we are going to learn about number sequence. Does anyone know what that means?" The children mumbled amongst themselves for a moment. Willaim's hand went up.

"Yes, William." The boy stood up, he looked uneasy now that the others were looking at him.

"Order Miss Mary?" Mary smiled at him, nodding to the boy to take his seat.

"That's quite right William. Order, for everything, must have its order. Why? Because if we didn't have order in things, we would simply be in a muddle and that would never do."

The class went well, David trying especially hard and not losing his temper once.

In the study, Mary filled Elsbeth in on the morning's work. She was pleased that David had engaged in the lesson, he could be difficult when it came to math.

"Of course we have Captain Freddie to thank for this, you must convey my thanks to the man."

Elsbeth agreed.

"He came to see David only a few days ago. Such a pleasant man and the child quite obviously loves him."

Mary had not met the man, she had heard his name many times in the last few weeks.

"Is he indeed. I imagine you are all bowled over by the hero that returned David." Her voice had a slight laugh in its tone.

"Mary! Whatever are you inferring? The man simply wanted to keep in touch with the child, I see no harm in it. He is very fond of David, as we all are."

"Now, we must talk about Doris. I feel, should the situation go on without our intervention, well, she might never speak again. What are your thoughts?"

Elsbeth placed her head in her hands, she had gone over this time and again and honestly was at her witts end with what to do.

"I agree, however, we cannot force the child to talk. I don't know what to do Mary, really I don't. If I knew what sparked it, maybe then I could begin to work on the issue. The simple truth is I don't."

"Can you remember the day that she last spoke? Maybe we could figure out if anything in particular happened?"

Elsbeth thought hard, she muttered words under her breath and stopped abruptly.

"Oh, dear Lord! What have I done." The woman fled from the room leaving a mystified Mary standing alone.

"Doris, Doris my love. Come here, my angel." Doris was sitting on the floor of the nursery, trusty teddy in hand. She looked over at the woman sitting on the edge of the bed.

"Come here, dear. I think you and I need to have a little talk."

Ruby appeared at the door. Her heart saddened when she watched the young child in all her bewildering ways. Elsbeth was about to send the girl away when she approached Doris.

"Give me your hand. Shall we sit on the cot? It's warm and comfy, come on. Let's sit next to Miss Elsbeth." Doris did as she was asked, taking Ruby's hand they made their way over to Elsbeth.

"There now, isn't that better." Smiled the girl. Doris nodded. From the corner of her eyes, she looked at Elsbeth. She hadn't once looked at her directly since she stopped talking, in all the fuss of the last months it had mostly gone unnoticed. She noticed now.

"How about we play a game, Doris?" Elsbeth wondered where the girl was going with this but let her continue, all the same, she was intrigued. Doris nodded.

"Why are you sad? Can Teddy tell me?" Doris raised the bear to Ruby's ear, her voice but a whisper as Teddy told Ruby all about the night that Miss Elsbeth got angry, that she did not want strangers in her house. Teddy continued in his whisper that David had gone, He and Doris might have to go too. Elsbeth sat back dismayed, it had never been her intention to have the child feel unwelcome.

"Teddy, can you tell Doris that I am truly sorry and she is not a stranger, this is her home too and Miss Elsbeth would never, ever make her leave. She would never send any of the children away. David was not sent away, somebody took him and it made Miss Elsbeth so very, very sad. So sad that she said things she did not mean to Miss Mary and Miss Grace."

Doris turned her head, she looked at Elsbeth for the first time in a long time.

"Promise?" she whispered. Pulling the child into her arms she wept quietly.

"I promise. Come here, Ruby." She pulled Ruby into the hug as the 3 of them sat there in the nursery. Ruby was not used to hugs, she liked them.

"When is Mr Tom coming back?" The woman was taken by surprise at the question.

"I don't know dear, do you miss him too?" Doris nodded her head, she did miss him. He made her laugh.

"Then we will have to do something about that, won't we?"

Esther was proving her worth as a housemaid to the children, she came from a large family herself, quite used to keeping the little ones in check. She had become friendly with the stablehand over the weeks she had been at the Hall, this pleased Elsbeth more than she could acknowledge. It was never the plan to cause the girl any issues, she simply wanted her away from Tom. A jealous snarling in her stomach that she didn't understand would rise whenever she saw the 2 together, still, that was not a problem now in light of Toms disappearing act. Where was he? If he knew that it was safe to return she was sure that he would, wouldn't he? Billoughby had mentioned that he had not stopped making his own discreet enquiries up and down the coast. These had come to nothing as yet, he continued regardless. He had to be somewhere, a person could not simply vanish. Elsbeth had even gone to the expense of hiring her own private detective, he had come highly recommended from Mr Braithwaite the solicitor. Mr Braithwaite had been a difficult man to convince at the off, he did not understand why a woman of her standing would go to such lengths to find a simple farmhand.

"I feel I owe it to the family." She had explained.

"They, the Inspector and his son, worked tirelessly to retrieve my ward and now I feel I simply must do all I can to do the same." He had grunted several times throughout the conversation, still, it was her money and not for the likes of him to tell her otherwise. And, so it was agreed. The man would do his utmost to find the chap and give him the news that his name was cleared of any wrongdoing.

Grace read the letter that had arrived from Janet and Henry. They had not seen each other since the wedding.

"How the devil are they?" inquired Billoughby.

"You will be able to judge that for yourself soon enough. They are coming to visit over Christmas, bringing Geraldine too. Oh, I have missed them."

"Do we have room?" Billoughby asked, having now converted the spare room into an office. He had been meaning to do this for some time, the house had always seemed too full.

"Geraldine will stay at the Hall, she has already spoken to Elsbeth about it. I thought we could put Henry and Janet in Adam's old room." Yes, that would work.

"Seems between you, you ladies have it all worked out nicely."

"You remember we are to have Christmas at the Hall dear? It will make a nice change not to have the cooking to do. I think it's Elsbeth's way of apologising, though I told her she has no need." Billoughby imagined it was more to do with all the children and too few adults at the place. There was something to be said about the adult company over the festive season.

"Will there be another village party this year?" Grace pondered the question for a while.

"Gracie?"

"I'm not sure, I've not heard anything about it if there is. I'll find out, I have to go over there this afternoon. The young Master Jacob is growing so fast, he's outgrown the clothes I made in a month! Can you believe that?"

"Boy's, remember ours? Didn't grow for ages then up to my shoulders." They laughed as the pair remembered their sons in their younger days.

"Do you want me to drop you up there on my way out?" He continued.

"That would be nice, dear. I don't need to leave yet, some lunch first I think."

Daisy got off the train, it seemed strange to be back in London after everything that had happened. She was to meet Julian at the tea rooms to discuss her plans.

She watched him from outside, sitting there in his smart suit. Goodness, but he was a handsome man.

"Coming in Miss?" asked the doorman politely. She nodded as he held the door open.

"Miss Harvey."

"Right this way Miss."

"Hello, you." He kissed her cheek warmly. This was no place for the bear hugs she had received when he came to visit.

"Sit, my dear, please do. Your journey was not too tiresome I hope?"

"Not at all, it was quite a pleasant change to sit by myself with time to read. How are you?"

Julian talked about the work he had been occupied with, the changes in staff that he had to train, the outings that he had to oversee. All very exciting, thought Daisy. They ordered tea and cakes. He stared at her, she had not noticed he had stopped talking.

"You are not coming to London, are you?" He was a good reader of people, he had to be in his job. Daisy shook her head.

"It is not that I don't want to be near you dearest Julian, I do. I feel London isn't the place for me. I escaped it once, I adore where I am and have no wish to leave it just yet."

"I can't say I'm shocked, having been to visit your quaint village, I too would have trouble leaving it. When you say 'be near me' is that the only reason you considered the position?"

"No, although it was one of the main reasons it wasn't the only reason."

"So you feel it too? This unspoken feeling?" The woman blushed, her face now crimson.

"My dear, are you going to faint again?"

"Heavens, no. I find all this talk a little unnerving if I'm honest. I do feel it, yes, but what are we to do?" Taking her hand in his he raised it to his lips, kissed it then placed it back on the table.

"Leave that to me, my wonderful Daisy."

They spent the rest of the afternoon walking through the park until it was time for Daisy to catch her train.

"I will be in touch soon. Will you wait for me?" Daisy was taken aback by the question.

"Of course I will. There has not nor will there be anyone else." Julian's face visibly relaxed as he held her close to his chest.

Twelve

It was Christmas Eve and Elsbeth had decided against another party at the house, instead, they had done as Mary asked and held a Christmas sale of sorts. Cate was in charge as it had been her idea initially. She was in her element at the amount they raised with people travelling from other villages to grab a bargain. The money was donated to the church and the needy, a small amount kept back to hold a party of sorts in the village hall. The trauma of the previous year's party had left too much of a bad memory in Elsbeth's mind. The party had been a great success, the children from the hall getting to meet the children from the village was of particular use. They would soon be integrated into the main school so it was a pleasant bonus that they were welcomed with curiosity and kindness in equal measure.

The bell rang out as the children were having breakfast. It was Mr Nash, he had vegetables to deliver for the coming Christmas day lunch. With him, he had 2 packages, one for David and another for Elsbeth.

"Whatever could they be?" She asked as he handed them to her.

"No idea Mrs Stanhope, thought, as I was coming this way I would drop them off for you."

Elsbeth took the packages into the library, the postmark on one said Portsmouth. This was the package for David and she imagined it would be from Freddie. The one addressed to her was difficult to make out as much as the postmark went. The writing on the label was not, she stared at it for a good while.

Sally knocked on the door of the library, Elsbeth had been less familiar with the woman since her talk with Billoughby. She wanted to discharge her if she was honest with herself, help was hard to find and that was Sally's only saving grace.

"Yes?" Sally entered the room, her eyes glancing at the parcels.

"Something nice?" asked the woman.

"Did you need something Sally?"

"Sorry, Ma'am. The children are ready for the church service, shall we stay here today?"

Elsbeth did not want the woman snooping any more than she already did in their absence.

"Not at all, you should come with us, it would be a help and this is a special service. The Reverend has worked hard on the Christmas services." Sally nodded.

"Right you are, Ma'am. We shall wait in the parlour."

"Could you ask David to come to me?" Sally left the room, minutes later David came through.

"David, we have a package here for you. Shall we place it under the tree and you could open it tomorrow?" David's eyes were wide. He had never had a package before.

"What is it, Miss Elsbeth?"

"Well, I don't know dear. I imagine it to be a present of some sort. Do you know anyone that may send you a present?" She smiled at the boy's quizzical face.

"No, Miss Elsbeth, ain't never had a package nor a present."

"Have not, dear, have not had a package."

David screwed up his face.

"Have not, Miss Elsbeth. It's big, isn't it?"

"It is, big enough to be an automobile do you think?" David laughed, she was silly.

"No, Miss Elsbeth. I don't think anyone would send me an automobile."

"Let us place it under the tree, I am sure we don't want to be late for Reverend Moore now, do we?" They carried the parcel into the hall, David pushing it carefully under the tree.

"Shall we put your package under the tree, Miss Elsbeth?"

"No, dear. It will be new notepapers I'm sure, not a thing that should be under a tree."

The church was brimming with people. Elsbeth, Sally, and Esther ushered the children in. They sat at the front as was their way. A small row of smaller chairs had been placed in front of them for the children. Christmas was a time that the children joined the congregation. The Reverend insisted on it, he would borrow chairs from the school and place them at the front on either side. The children of the village were growing up fast, making the children of the hall the smaller of the gathering. This would be the first service of the day with another later in the evening. The evening service would consist of singing Christmas hymns and carols followed by wine and fruit cake. It was the service that the Reverend Moore particularly enjoyed, he felt these small touches brought more people to the church, it was a joyous time after all.

Grace and Milton took their seat beside Janet and Henry, Grace reaching over to say hello to Geraldine. Adam was late, as he often was for these things. Cate could be heard chastising him as they made their way into the church.

"Morning, Ma. Sorry, Adam decided to change again, I ask you. Who is the woman in our house." Adam sat down, Maisy on his knee.

"I had to Ma, little Maisy threw her porridge at me, my shirt was sticky."

"You're here now dear. Aren't you a little one, throwing things at your Pa?" She laughed quietly as she stroked the child's face. The Reverend had a quick look around to make sure everyone that should be here was and began his service.

That night, Elsbeth carefully unwrapped the parcel in the privacy of her room. The outer packaging was of brown paper but she recognised the handwriting the moment she saw it. The day had been a long one, made even longer by the need to get a minute to herself that would bring her to discover what word there might be inside. Inside, the paper was a shiny gold one, expensive-looking, she thought. Carefully she untied the ribbon of red, she could feel the envelope even before it was unwrapped. The shawl was a beautifully crafted piece of work, with its fine silken threads that were woven between the soft wool, she held it to her face trying to catch the slightest of aroma from the person that had sent it. The envelope simply read, *Elsbeth*. Tearing it open, there on the paper was the news she had dreaded…

My Dearest Elsbeth,
I have thought long and hard about what to say to you. I am safe and as well as I can be. You must know that I have nothing to do with David's disappearance, I would never do anything to harm you or the child. I know what they are saying about me in the

village, that is why I felt I must get away. In time I hope the child finds his way back to you. I have not contacted Father, I fear this may put him and my family in a difficult situation. I have been working so have made enough to get by on. The job is not what I have been used to but it's a living for the time being. I sat at the edge of your gardens before I left, I saw you with the man, I presume he is a close friend and I wish you both only good things, be happy my dearest Elsbeth, for there is no one that deserves it more, he looked a kindly chap and I dare say he will treat you well. There was never anything between the girl and myself, please believe that. You were then and always will be my heart. I plan to take the liner when it launches and try to begin a new life overseas without you. I wish you every happiness, my love,
Tom.

The paper soaked up each tear that dropped onto it. How could he not have seen David? What was she to do, for it would surely not be a letter that could be shown to the Inspector? They would never understand. Wrapping the shawl around her shoulders she wept quietly, alone once more.

The liner, what did he mean? Surely he did not intend to take the ship that Adam had worked on, how? From what she had heard the tickets were expensive enough for those with money. When did it launch? She must find out.

The children woke early that next morning, it was to be their first Christmas in the Hall. Esther helped to get them all ready for the day, she was to spend the day with her parents once her tasks were complete. Geraldine smiled as she watched the small group eat their breakfast, excited at what the day had to bring.

"Look at them, they are adorable. Are you excited children?" They nodded as they gulped down food, eager to get to the presents. They had not had the luxury of presents in their young lives, most of them had not had proper meals so this was indeed a special day.

They had wandered around the large tree in the hall for days now, trying to guess what could possibly be wrapped in the seemingly endless piles of presents. Mary had been most impressed that not a 1 of them had tried to open any.

"How do they do it? When I was a child I would have tried opening at least 1 or 2, they are a credit, they really are." She had remarked to

Elsbeth. Elsbeth agreed, she too had far too much curiosity as a child and often was playfully chastised for trying to peek.

Elsbeth's parents arrived mid-morning, accompanied by her brother Jon and his wife with their children. The house was beginning to fill as more guests made their appearance. It was with regret that Renton had written to say they could not join them, one of the children had a bout of influenza and they felt it unwise to travel, or, spread the illness further afield. Secretly Mary was glad that they wouldn't be coming, not that she wished harm on the child, she simply could not feel at ease with a person that was so alike to her deceased brother and that was the truth of it.

"We shall wait for the Inspector and Grace, they should be here soon. I have given the children a present each to keep them amused until we are all here. It didn't seem right to have them waiting around."

"Dear, you are making a rod for your own back." Laughed Elsbeth's mother.

"I am sure I won't mother, they have been so patient I thought it only fair."

Sitting on the floor in the parlour the children each played with the toy that they had unwrapped. The girl's had doll's, doll's with different hair colours so that they wouldn't get mixed up. Elsbeth knew this may be something that could cause an issue from her days working in the school, she was not about to let that happen. The boys had spinning tops, hoop games and toy soldiers made of wood. They were content, it was plain to see.

The adults sat and watched the young ones, drinking tea and eating sandwiches as they admired how well-behaved they were.

Grace and Billoughby entered the parlour, arms laden with packages and pre-cooked dishes.

"Geraldine, dear, could you help me set these down somewhere?"

"Of course Grace, come this way. We can put the dishes in the dining hall and the parcels under the tree. Hello, Cate, Adam. Oo, little Maisy, my you are growing fast." Geraldine helped Grace unload her arms, Billoughby went straight in to sit with the children.

"What have we got here? That never is a soldier."

The child laughed, the old man was funny. Of course, it was a soldier! Just like the one's that guarded the King and Queen.

Cate and Adam arrived within minutes of his parents, closely followed by Mary and Robert. They had kindly picked the Reverend Moore up on their way. The man looked positively freezing as he made his way to the open fire.

"Reverend, no Daisy with you?" Asked Billoughby.

"No, she sends her regards and best wishes but has chosen to return home to see her parents. My guess is that she will fit in a visit to her young chap, can't say that I blame her, young bright thing that she is." He smiled fondly as Geraldine came to stand by his side.

"Hello, dear. Wonderful service you gave, well done you."

"Thank you, I try to keep it jovial at this time of the year, especially when we have the youngsters joining us. It doesn't do to put them off, don't you agree?"

Geraldine nodded, handing the Reverend a steaming hot mug of tea.

"I do indeed Tobias, there are far too many things in life that are dreadful, the church should spread the joys and wonders when it can."

"No news of Tom?" Asked Elsbeth quietly, for she did not want to overplay her concern.

"No, she doesn't say it but I know my Gracie is half out of her mind with worry."

"I can well imagine, it must be so difficult, the not knowing. What do you think he will do Inspector?" Billoughby scratched his head, looking around at the group he leant forward so as not to be heard.

"My guess is, he has no clue the lad is home so will get as far away as he can. If only I could get word to him, tell him he is safe to come home. Yes, I know he does this to spare his mother and me but just a clue as to his whereabouts, that's all I ask."

This wasn't altogether what she wanted to hear, Elsbeth felt bad enough that she knew he was safe but could say nothing. What was she to do?

Dinner was served, the table was as beautiful as could be. Many houses would have the children seated at a smaller table, not in this house, each child was to take their seat between the adults. Jacob stared at the feast that lay before them, his eyes began to fill up, as much as he tried to fight the overwhelming emotion he could not.

"Are you okay, young fella." Asked Robert at seeing the silent tears roll.

"Never had me a Christmas dinner before." Robert patted the boy gently across his shoulder.

"Truth of it is, and I am a truthful one lad, never had me a Christmas dinner like this before, either. It's a sight to see, fair takes my breath. See, the way I'm thinking is this, we best make sure we tuck in and make the most of it, yes?"

Jacob managed a small laugh.

"Yes, Sir."

"That's the spirit, Now, let's say a little prayer and a thank you to him upstairs."

Reverend Moore said a few words of thanks before they made their onslaught of the magnificent feast that sat before them.

Mary listened with interest to the conversation of Adam and Geraldine, Adam was talking about the great liner that he had worked on. Geraldine asked if the young man was not a little tempted to take a trip on the ship he had put so much work into.

"Lord, no. Cate would have my hide, I aim to settle down here and raise a family, my travelling days are well behind me. I had the opportunity, of course, I did."

"In what way?"

"Some of us workers were given a round trip ticket, myself included."

"Goodness, how lucky, I hear they are selling out fast if not already sold."

"As I said, I won't be using it. I gave it to my brother."

The clatter of the serving spoon hitting the glassware brought the table to a hush.

"You did what?" Elsbeth could not stop the words from coming out. Adam could feel all eyes on him now, when would he learn to keep quiet!

It was Grace that got out of her chair, Elsbeth's comment already lost in the woman's mind.

"When did you give it to him? Did he take it with him, do you know? Oh, Son! Why did you not tell us this?" Adam shook his head.

"I didn't think Ma. I don't know if he took it with him, I'm sorry, I just didn't think."

Billoughby took Grace's hand, leading her back to her chair and sitting her back down.

"Now, children, wasn't that a bit of a to-do? Grown-ups, eh! They will miss all this nice hot food if they're not careful so let's us make a start and leave grown-up talk for a day that isn't Christmas day." The Inspector glared around the table at the adults, a warning to let this go for the time being.

"Yes, well said Inspector. Fill your plates children, plenty to get through."

The meal went exceptionally well, Grace and Elsbeth both with their minds racing yet heeding the warning to get the day back on track for the children's sakes. Billoughby talked at length with William and Ruby. Did they enjoy the house and the countryside, were they looking forward to starting at the big school after Christmas? William talked of his life before they moved to the hall, he was emphatic in his happiness at his new life in the hall.

"I went to the poorhouse a long time ago, my mother and father left me there. It was cold and dirty and we never had anything like the food we have here." Billoughby nodded, he could not imagine the things that these children had been through, he looked over to Elsbeth. What a wonderful, kind-hearted woman she was to have opened her home and to do it without asking for anything in return. She looked tired, he thought. He imagined it was not the extra children that caused this, something else, but what?

"I want to go to school." Said Ruby in her timid voice.

"I hear you are all very clever children, the local children are nice, you will enjoy it."

Tom ate his meal with the family he was staying with, it was very kind of them to invite him. They had noticed he didn't speak of his own family at all so assumed he had none. The occasion was a relaxed one, he thought about his mother and father now. He would have dearly loved to see them once more before he left England, as he would his Elsbeth, his brother and family. But no, that was out of the question.

Heading back to his room after dinner he sat on his bed with a notepad and pencil. Could he dare write to them now or should he wait until he was securely on the ship? Maybe he could put a line to Adam, he could ask that he keeps it to himself until the time is right? His head was spinning with what to do for the best. Placing the notepad back on the small side-table he decided to wait. Tom grabbed his coat from the back of the door, he needed to walk and clear his mind.

"Can I join you?" Turning in surprise Tom was met with the son of his employers.

"I'm heading down to the seafront, you'll need a heavy coat it's cold out there, that wind is picking up a fair bit." The young man held his coat up and smiled.

"Always prepared. You have to be when you've lived close to the sea for as long as I have."

The 2 men walked for a time, quietly at first. It was dark now as the nights drew in fast during the winter months on the coast. Tom pulled his coat tighter around himself.

"Do you plan to take over the Inn in time?"

"It's what my father would like, I dare not tell him I have other idea's. I want to see the world, Stan. You know? Before I have to settle down, there are so many more opportunities out there."

"Your parents would not approve?" The man shook his head, carefully finding his footing on the uneven ground beneath his feet.

"Father says my place is here, he keeps a tight rein on my pay, you can't travel the world on good looks alone, my friend!" He laughed. He was a good-looking man too, there was no denying this. He had a delicate, almost high-born look to him. He was a hard worker, there was no doubt about that as Tom had seen for himself, it was little wonder they didn't want to lose him to travel. In any other circumstances, the 2 would have made for great friends, Tom felt it unwise to make such relationships as he did not plan to stay for too much longer.

"Do you have a special lady, Stan?" The question caught the young farmer off-guard, what was he to say? Yes, I have one, she is twice my age and widowed 2 times over. Instead, Tom looked out to the brightness of the moon and sighed.

"No, no one special, just me. How about you, is there someone you have your eye on?"

The man shook his head, he too not about to admit the feelings he had for a person that was out of his grasp.

"Too busy at work, that's our problem, Stan." He laughed, a laugh that was not a convincing one in Tom's mind.

"It's a good, bright moon up there tonight. I came down here 2 nights ago and you could barely see one foot in front of the other."

"Yes, I saw you leave the Inn, I did wonder where you were going in the dark. Man of mystery, eh, Stan?" This time his laugh was genuine as the pair made their way over the sandy beach.
They walked for some time, the fresh winter breeze getting colder.
"Time to head back I think, that wind's picking up."
"After you, you can shield me from the blasts."

The Inn was gloriously warm when they returned, with the large fire ablaze they huddled around the bright naked flames.
"Mad, that's what you youngsters are! Walking out in the dark is bad enough but, in this weather, I ask you." Grumbled the Innkeeper as he took his seat next to the roaring inferno.
"It's good for you Father, a nice walk after a rested day would do you the world of good."
"I'll have to take your word on that son, 20 years ago perhaps, not now with my knee."
"What happened to your knee, Sir?" Asked Tom. He noticed the man limped slightly but had never asked him why.
"That's from his war days Stan, a bit of a hero my dad."
"We were all heroes son, I was one of the lucky ones. They only got my leg, some didn't make it back at all."
Tom nodded, he had heard his father and the Reverend talk quietly over the last year about their time in the war, it did not sound as exciting as some would think, it sounded horrific.
The man continued, his voice low and shaky.
"I never thought that people could do such things to each other, but they do, see, they're same as you or me in a funny way, fighting because they're ordered to and it's you or them. We all had families that we wanted to get back to, some made it, some did not on both sides."
He supped what was left in his mug, patted his son on the head and headed off to bed.
"Don't be up all night lads, busy day tomorrow." He called behind him.

The 2 men talked a while longer, mostly about the area and people that lived in it. The lad told of the school he had attended here in his younger days, the friends he had made that now, one by one, seemed to have married with children of their own.

"It's a strange feeling like I've been standing still while the world spins on around me. Do you understand, Stan?" Tom nodded, he had long had this same feeling, more so since Adam had arrived back home. A feeling he was waiting for something to happen, mind you, something did happen didn't it!

"You know there's a world out there, you yearn to see it. I doubt you will ever settle until you have satisfied yourself that you tried. Right, that's me for my bed. Good talking, it was nice." Tom left the young man sitting alone in front of the fire and went to bed.

Up in his room, Tom stared at the ticket that he had pulled from his box. What that young fella downstairs would give for this chance he thought to himself and here he was, not more than 3 months away from setting off on the adventure of a lifetime. It was not an adventure he had planned on pursuing that was for sure. Truth be told he had fully intended to sell the ticket for he was certain there would be plenty out there that would jump at the chance. It seemed inevitable that he would now have need of it, this was a mess there would be no getting out of. Tom safely tucked it back in the box, sliding it under the floorboard he pulled the covers over himself and drifted off to sleep.

The day had been a wonderfully festive occasion that the children had thoroughly enjoyed. Tucking the covers around baby Dolly, Elsbeth kissed her gently on the forehead.

"Sleep well little one, it has been a busy day for you." She walked over to where Doris lay, clutching her raggedy teddy to her chest, her breath quiet and even. Elsbeth stroked the stray hair from the child's face, she did not stir. It wasn't often that the children stayed up so late, today had been a special day for all of them. Each, and every one of them had fallen asleep within minutes of climbing into their cots, all content as children should be. Reverend Moore had left earlier with Mary and Robert. He had drunk far too much Sherry and although he wasn't a boisterous man it was felt wise to take him home where he could sleep it off. The children found the sight of the Reverend being tipsy highly amusing. Grace and Milton left shortly after, taking Adam and Cate with them. Geraldine had gone to bed leaving Elsbeth's parents and sibling along with Janet and Henry, downstairs. The group was a jovial one when she rejoined them. They were all to stay the night, it felt good to have the house full.

"Did the little one's go off to sleep okay, dear?"

"In minutes, Mother. They must have been so tired, it's been quite a day for them."

"You made it a wonderful day for them, dear. We are so proud of you."

"Oh, Father, they deserve to have a wonderful time, they have known so little happiness in their short lives."

"Today, I think we can all agree, you gave them exactly that." Elsbeth's brother stood, drink in hand.

"To my dearest sister, you are indeed an angel. To Elsbeth." The group raised the glasses, Elsbeth turning quite red at the unexpected toast.

"I could not have done this without your support, all of you."

"Now, the only thing left to do is find you a suitable Father figure for these children, they need a firm figure in their lives, as do you dear."

Elsbeth frowned, she loved her Father dearly, yet at times he could say the most expected things.

"We can manage perfectly well as we are, father dear."

The new year came with everyone bustling about the village at a slower rate than normal, it was cold, the red rosy faces did not stop for their usual bouts of gossip in the lanes as they did in the warmer months. For Grace and Billoughby it was agonising, as good as the Inspector was at his job he could not seem to locate his son. The couple often had quiet conversations about where he could be, would he use the ticket? They had resigned themselves to the fact that they would have to wait it out until the day of the launch.

"There's nothing more we can do, Gracie. I've looked everywhere I can to find the lad, he's not daft that one, he will keep right out of the way. We just have to be patient."

Grace was patient, this was her baby boy they were talking about and all patience that she had once had, had fled.

"Could we put an advert in the paper, Milton? If he saw that it was safe to come home I know he would." Milton shook his head in despair, he pulled out a pile of cutting's from his breast pocket.

"Look, I didn't want to get your hopes up, my love, I have put many adverts in the papers over the months. We've had nothing back." Grace hugged her husband, she had no idea that he had gone to these lengths.

"What's that for?"

"Because I love you. I have not been charitable to you, now you show me these."

"I want the boy home as much as you do, I think our best chance is to go to Southampton a day before the ship sail's, see if we can't find our lad."

Grace had to agree it was the best thing to do, however much 3 months seemed a lifetime away.

Daisy was surprised to see Julian standing at the door of the Rectory.

"Are you going to let me in woman, it's positively freezing out there."

"When did you get here, did you write me of your visit? I did not get a letter."

Julian grabbed the startled woman into a hug, his face felt cold but his well-wrapped body did not.

"Can't a chap surprise his soon to be fiance?"

"Shh, the Reverend will hear you, I haven't told anybody."

"Why not? Are you ashamed of me Miss Harvey?" He laughed.

"Of course not, silly. I thought it only right that we announce it together. My, the Inspector will be shocked to hear the news, likely think he will be looking for a new Constable."

"Nonsense, he has a perfectly marvellous Constable right here."

This made Daisy smile, even more, she loved that Julian had no issues with her career and her wanting to continue on her path.

"Did I hear...Oh, hello, do come inside and warm yourself. Daisy, you didn't mention a visit."

"I didn't know, Reverend."

"I thought I would surprise you, hello Reverend. How are you?"

"I'm jolly good dear boy, how the devil are you? Are you staying in the village?"

Julian nodded, removing his coat he walked into the warm parlour.

"I am, for a few days at any rate. I am well thank you, could do with some warmer days of course but where would we be without the seasons and all that they bring?"

"Quite right, quite right. Will you be staying at the Inn?"

Julian grinned, his face almost bursting.

"No, I shall be staying at a beautiful little cottage. Daisy, this afternoon I would be delighted if you would walk with me to give it your approval, as you will be mostly living in it after..."

"After what?" Insisted Tobias.

Julian tapped his nose as he laughed.

"All will become clear, now, did I hear talk of a hot drink. My bones are quite frozen."

Tobias was intrigued, he poured the tea into the mugs as he played over in his mind what the man could mean. Perhaps he wanted Daisy to housesit? Marriage would not work, not with the distance between them and Daisy having turned down the post in London. Tobias had known many a couple over the years that had tried to continue a marriage whilst separated and it simply did not work in his book.

"There we are, get your hands around that. Now, do tell, what brings you here?"

Thirteen

It was the first sign of Spring, the small Daffodil swayed gently in the breeze. A delicate thing yet it stood strong against the wind that blew across the field. Grace smiled as she watched it for a while. Not only was it a sign of warmth to come but a sign that it would soon be time for them to make a trip to find their son. He had been gone, what seemed an age now and she missed him terribly. She missed their early morning talks in the depths of winter, where the pair would be the only ones awake in the cottage. She missed watching him fall asleep after a long day at the farm in the armchair next to the fire, mostly she just missed knowing her boy was safe and well.

"Grace?" Turning around she was surprised to see Robert.

"Hello there, what brings you this way?" Robert would normally be in full swing on the farm at this time of day.

"You know, it was one of those mornings that I decided to simply take a walk. We've been hold-up at the farm over the winter with not many walks, I felt like walking today. Look, even the Daf has come out, Spring is on its way thank the heavens."

"Yes, I have been admiring it. Funny how it's such a tiny thing, yet it battles against the wind admirably. How is Mary? I have been meaning to call, as you say, it's been too cold."

"Mary is well, keeping herself busy with some of the children from the hall. It's not the same without him, is it?" Grace realised that she wasn't the only one that missed Tom.

"No, I suppose you have noticed it too, that strange quietness where he used to be. Not a loud man by any means but his lack of presence is overwhelming at times."

"Best worker I ever had. I hope he comes back soon, love. Adam is a fine man, solid worker 'an all, Tom and I, well we were mates. I miss the lad Grace, I truly do."

"Milton and I are going to Southampton soon, I pray that Tom will be there, that we can bring him home."

"Young David keeps asking over him, every time he comes to the farm with Mary. Don't know what to tell the lad. If you need anything, or I can be of help with your trip, please let me know. I'll tell Mary you were asking over her, bye Grace love." Robert continued on his walk, his figure getting smaller to Grace's eye as he strode across the field and out of sight.

Daisy had settled into the cottage quickly, putting her own touches to it here and there. Grace had helped out with furnishings, Daisy insisting on paying the woman for her wonderful work. Grace was a proud woman, she took some persuading. Eventually, Daisy pointed out that it would come in handy if their Granddaughter needed anything, Grace relented. Julian came over to the cottage every 2 weeks, much to the Reverend's dismay.

"It simply doesn't do to have you both stay under the same roof, unchaperoned and unmarried, Daisy. What will people say?" Daisy cocked her head to one side.

"They will say whatever they want to say, Tobias, I have long since stopped worrying about village gossip. We have separate room's, they are welcome to look though I won't be inviting them to. We are doing nothing untoward and if they cannot take my word for that, then so be it."

Tobias despaired, he wanted what was best for the young woman and knew how some of the locals could spin a tale as long as their arm. Daisy would not be swayed.

That afternoon she baked up a storm, it had been good practice living at the Rectory and Tobias never complained about the meals she served him.

"There, try that." She placed the plate before the Reverend triumphantly. The hot filling of apples and blackberries sending bursts of fruity aroma's around the room.

"How can I argue with such a wonderful cook, you put me at a disadvantage, my dear."

Her laughter told the Reverend that she was well aware of this, as he eagerly pushed the spoon into his mouth.

"This is simply incredible, my dear girl. I shall miss your baking."

Daisy shrugged, she had not said that she would no longer cook for the Reverend.

"Are you going away, Tobias?"

"No, not me dear girl. I had assumed that once you and Julian were married you would no longer be in a position to tend to this old man's needs."

"Oh, you are silly. I have to cook, it will be no trouble to continue to do so for you. It isn't like you're a long way from here, practically next door!" The smile on his face showed his relief, he had wondered if he would have to employ a person. Not that he begrudged doing this, no, he had come to favour the woman's meals over most that he had tasted.

"I am so pleased to hear that, I was bracing myself to have a word with Sally and after all that business with young Tom, I was not looking forward to it."

"I have to admit, it surprised me that she was so vicious about the whole incident and more so that she has remained at the hall. Mrs Stanhope surely has more reserve than I would have had."

"I imagine she has to be, a strong woman and no mistake, she has suffered so many blows in her lifetime it must thicken one's skin." Daisy nodded, she knew what she would have done. Still, at least Mrs Stanhope was aware of the woman's ways.

"I imagine April can't come quickly enough for the Inspector and Grace. I do so hope they find Tom."

"Yes, although I did warn them that it will be very busy the day that ship sails, they'll have to keep their eyes peeled if they are to spot him amongst the many people that will turn up simply to watch its departure!"

"I don't think anything will deter them. They are so desperate to have word from him."

Elsbeth pushed the letter deep into her skirt pocket, it was the second time she had received that familiar handwriting and her heart skipped a beat when Sally handed it to her.

"Anyone, we know?" Asked the housemaid in her usual inquisitive way.

"I imagine if it were your business, Sally, it would be addressed to you." That was the end of that conversation.

In the kitchen, the woman hissed her venomous thoughts to the cook.

"Fancy fella I reckon, she doesn't need to be so lardy dah about it, I was only asking out of politeness. Damn near tore my head off my shoulders she did too!" The cook sighed, too long had she listened to the woman and her theories about the Missus, a quiet woman she had had enough.

"Why don't you keep your beak out of that which doesn't concern you, Sally. Always moaning about this and that, Lord, if the woman has a fancy fella, good luck to her I say. Heart of gold that one and you mind what I say now, carry on and you will be looking for a new place of work. You got it cushy here, don't you forget that." Sally was stunned, she had never been spoken to in that way before by the cook, she had a mind to report the woman.

"You can't speak to me like that. I have a right to my thoughts same as anyone else around here."

"Then keep them like that, thoughts, nobody wants to hear them."

Esther could hear the woman's voices from the hallway.

"Keep it down you 2, can hear you out there. Sally, the little ones need fetching from school soon. Are you to walk with me, it's a nice day today I thought we could walk back and give them some exercise. Mrs Stanhope could do with 5 minutes, nipper had her up again last night with her teeth poor little mite."

"Better than listening to any more nonsense from this one!" Barked Sally at the cook.

Billoughby was out on a call from one of the local farmer's when he bumped into Mr Nash. The grocer was climbing back into his cart after delivering to the Thompson house.

"How do, Inspector. What's happening in your world."

"Mr Nash, it's good to see you. I called to visit the old farm, seems a few sheep have gone missing. I could have sent the Constable but I quite fancied the walk."

"' Aye, not the first time this year either. I hear there's a group of roaming folk settled down near the Marsh, not that I'm saying it's them, mind, other's are though." Billoughby had heard this also, like Mr Nash, he wasn't convinced it had anything to do with them as they were usually quite mindful in the places they stayed.

"They don't often take from the place they're staying, worth checking in with them, no doubt. How's your good lady?"

"She's the same as ever, thanks, Inspector. Still cursing at the hours I have to work to keep us afloat. Some things never change, doubt I would recognise her if she did." He laughed.

"True enough, true enough. I promised I would call in to see my granddaughter on the way back, my but she's growing fast, they don't stay babies long do they?"

"No, they don't. Any news yet? On your lad I mean, seems he's been gone a long time now Inspector." Billoughby shook his head.

"Wish I could say different but, nothing to report there. Grace and I will be going over Southampton way to see if we can't spot him early April, can't come quick enough Mr Nash."

"If that bloody woman hadn't interfered he'd likely still be here. Shame there's no law about people that gossip too much in my opinion."

"The jails would be full Mr Nash! Right-o, best let you on your way. See you soon my friend."

Billoughby tapped on the cottage door, he could hear Cate singing inside. She called out for him to come in.

"Hello, love. How are you doing? Is Adam still working?"

"We are fine and dandy, aren't we little one? Come say hello to Grandpa." She picked the young child from the rug and handed her to the Inspector.

"Hello, little Maisy, my you get taller every time I see you."

"Adam will be home soon. Tea?"

"Tea would be lovely, dear. I'm parched after the walking I've done today. Are you ready for your visitors?" Cate shook her head, the expression on her face changing from a smile to a grimace.

"Oh, I'm not and no mistake, Sir. I can hear my Ma now, fetch me this, carry me that, we had such a terrible journey our Catey." Billoughby laughed at the mimicking woman.

"Oh, child, your Ma does that so well, doesn't she?" Maisy cooed her agreement with the man.

"Are they that bad?"

"You have no idea, I've had a 6-page letter about the trouble they've had trying to get a body in to look after the shop so I have. I didn't ask them to visit, told them so I did, wait until summer and we'll come to visit you. But, no. Ma wouldn't have it, gives her no reason to complain I'm sure."

"Parents, Cate. They need to feel it's them that does all the giving. How's this little one?"

"Ah, she's a delight so she is, not in the middle of the night I have to say. Been a bit cranky these past nights, had her in the bed with us twice this week. It seems to settle the little love down but not ideal in the long run of things."

"Do you think she's sickening for something?"

"I don't know to be truthful, fine in the day or so she seems. Adam thinks it's her teeth or the change in weather."

"I hear the little one at the hall has had a few restless nights too, maybe it's a bug, keep an eye on her. The doctor is only down the lane if you need him."

"I'm more along the lines that Adam is fretting about his brother and she senses it, him working all day and she's fine in the day. The closer it gets to April, the more he seems to worry in case you miss Tom. Can't speak for the hall and baby Dolly." Billoughby looked at his daughter-in-law, my she was a smart girl, a good thinker. Put him in mind of his Gracie, she would never have over fussed with the boys, instead, she would work things through methodically and be mostly right!

Adam pushed the door open, tugging off his boots before entering the parlour.

"Evening my lovelies, Pa, what a nice surprise. Is everything okay?"

"It is son, I promised Maisy here that I would pay her a visit, so here I am. How are you faring son?"

"Busy, but good thanks Pa. Robert has brought in a few extra lads to help out. How's Ma? Feels a while since I've seen you both."

"Your Ma's good, getting impatient for April as you can imagine. Looking forward to meeting Cate's parents too, she's filled the pantry up with all kinds of things that I'm not to touch."

"Lucky I'm not there, you know me and food, especially Ma's food. We can't wait, can we Cate?" Cate pulled a face behind her husband that made Billoughby chuckle.

"We cannot, dear. It cannot come too soon!"

Elsbeth sat in the study, the letter rustled in her pocket. She was dreading opening it for fear of what it might say. Maybe he had gone earlier on a cargo ship, this was possible, men did this all the time from what she had heard from Freddie. Her private detective had found not a shred of news on Tom and he had come highly recommended, Billoughby himself had pulled in many favours to have come up empty-handed. The postmark was, as the other times, smudged, making it impossible to ascertain the area, and even if it hadn't, there would be no telling it was posted from that place. Ruby knocked on the study door, her little face shining as it poked around into view.

"Hello, dearest. Please come in. You look happy, did you have a good day at school today?" Ruby nodded, in her hand was a piece of paper. She handed it to Elsbeth, her shy face glowing. Elsbeth opened up the paper, her eyes scanning it.

"Oh, my word! What a clever girl you are. Well done Ruby, I am so proud of you. Did you show this to anyone else?" Ruby shook her head.

"Would you mind if I do?" Again, the child shook her head.

"Come here, my dear." Elsbeth hugged the child tight.

"Hello, Miss Elsbeth. I am glad it is Saturday tomorrow. Miss Mary said I may go to the farm if it is okay for you?" David danced around at the door, he had wanted to run all the way home but was prevented from doing so by Sally and Esther.

"David, do you need to go to the W.C?" The boy was clearly having trouble concentrating as he danced around in the hall/

"Yes, Miss Elsbeth. But I wanted to tell you first."

"David, go and do what you need to, then come back and we shall discuss the farm."

"Yes, Miss." He flew from the hall to the washroom next to the kitchen, knowing he would never make the stairs.

"Isn't he an excitable boy, Ruby?" The pair giggled as they waited for his return.

After supper, Elsbeth asked everyone to stay at the table.

"We have some good news. Who would like to hear it?" The children cheered having no idea what it could possibly be.

"Ruby dear, stand up. Ruby has been chosen to play the piano at the Spring assembly. Isn't that wonderful, children. I think we should all give Ruby a round of applause to say a special, well done." The young child grinned back as the children clapped, they each felt it was very good news. They had all, at some point over the past months, heard Ruby play her soft tunes on the piano, they were in awe.

It wasn't until later that night, that Elsbeth noticed the date of the Spring assembly. It was to be Tuesday morning, the 9th of the month. This was going to be an issue, for she dearly wanted to see the young child perform her first time and give her all the support she so deserved, but what of her Tom? Could she make the journey in such a short space of time, she knew that if she could only have the chance to explain he would come back to her, wouldn't he? If the Spring assembly was only moved to another day. Maybe she could speak to the Head of the school, after all, she knew the man well having worked there for as long as she did. Yes, that is what she must do. On Monday morning she would accompany the children to school and put this suggestion forward. She pulled the letter from her pocket.

My darling,
I hope this letter finds you in good health. The place I am staying at the moment has had a few cases of fever. I am hoping with all my heart that you are not seeing any of this disease in the village. I hope that you and your new companion are well suited. I must confess, I thought long and hard before writing to you again. It is not my plan to upset your new arrangement, I want you to be happy my dearest Elsbeth, and if not with me then I take comfort that you were able to find this with another. I pray that David has been returned to you, I pray for this every night. The time is fast approaching where I am to leave these shores and England, forever. I will do so with a heavy heart. If you could be with me it would make all of this worthwhile, I know you cannot. Think of me fondly, as I do you. Keep a watch over my family, I know they will not understand and I cannot yet let them know of my whereabouts. This I entrust to you, my only love. One day, when this is far in the past, I hope to return to this green land that holds my heart.
Your Tom x

So he still planned to go, that was certain.

"I'm off now Ma'am, is there anything you need before I go?"
Elsbeth tucked the letter back into her pocket.
"No, thank you, Sally. We shall see you on Monday?"
"Yes, Monday, Ma'am. Good night."
Elsbeth walked along the corridor of the now quiet house. The children safely tucked up in bed. Esther had, as she often did these day's, gone out for a stroll with the stablehand. They were striking up quite the romance, it would come as no surprise if the 2 were to

announce a union at some point in the coming months. She had been harsh with the girl at the start, now she valued her input with the children immeasurably. Truth being that she could not have managed with the newer children without Esther's help and solid ways. Yes, she was definitely worth her weight. She thought about Tom's line where he spoke of the fever, it was a worry to everyone. Renton had written about it not a week ago. He was seeing cases daily in his work, that said he visited some terribly unsanitary places. He had warned Elsbeth and Mary of the symptoms and asked them not to take any unnecessary chances. Reverend Moore had also spoken of the poorhouses he had not been permitted to enter for this very reason. He had no alternative but to stay away. Elsbeth and he had sent parcels of extra food and clean blankets, there seemed little else they could do.

The woman checked around the house once more, retiring to her bed she reread the letter from Tom before drifting off to sleep. Her dreams, taking her to a warm and sandy place where they were unknown and free to love each other without retribution.

It was dark when the child's screams woke her. Rushing to the nursery in a bid to soothe her before the whole house was woken, Elsbeth lifted Dolly from the cot.

"Oh, there, there. My poor lamb, whatever is the matter that you scream so loudly. You're wet through little one." The child sobbed, her cheeks hot and red to touch. The child continued to cry, so much so, that Doris pushed back her covers and climbed from her bed.

"Did we wake you, little one? I think poor Dolly may have been having a bad dream. Would you like to sleep in my bed tonight?" Doris nodded, she stroked her sister's face gently, looking up at Elsbeth her face frowning.

"She's very hot, isn't she dear?" Doris nodded, her sister was burning hot.

"Would you like to do a little task for me?"

"Yes." Came the quiet voice, barely audible above the baby's screams.

"Run along over to Miss Esther's room, ask her to come to me in the nursery would you dear? Then you may go to my room and get yourself back to sleep."

Doris kissed her sister's hot brow before going to fetch the housemaid. The stairs went up to the attic rooms, it was dimly lit along the walls. She tapped softly at first on the door, there came no reply. Once again she tapped, louder this time but still no reply came. Turning the handle she pushed the heavy door open, she could make out the housemaid asleep in her bed. Approaching the bed she could hear murmurs from the young woman. Doris stretched up her hand and shook the hot shoulder, it felt damp just like Dolly's skin. Esther stirred, struggling to sit up she whispered hoarsely to the child.

"Doris, lovey what are you doing up here, couldn't you sleep?" Esther began to cough causing Doris to jump back. It was a rasping sound that the child had not heard before. Esther slumped back against her pillow, unable to muster the strength to sit up.

From the doorway, Doris could hear the baby's cries, followed by Miss Elsbeth.

"Doris, are you up there, dear? Did you wake Miss Esther?" Doris made her way back down the stairs to where Elsbeth stood.

"Miss Esther is sick." She said, her sweet little face now looking decidedly worried.

"Oh, dear me. Go and wash your hands dear, wash them well and then get off to sleep. Can you manage on your own Doris?" The child nodded, though why she had to wash her hands in the middle of the night was beyond her. Still, she did as was asked. Elsbeth's bed took a while for the little girl to climb onto, it was higher than her own cot and so much bigger. It felt warm from where the woman had laid in it. Doris snuggled up to her teddy and drifted back off to sleep. Elsbeth made her way up the stairs to where Esther was coughing.

"It's only me, Esther. How are you dear? Doris tells me you are not feeling at all well. The little one here seems to have the same sickness." Esther tried to sit, she had never had the Missus come up here before.

"Stay where you are dear, don't try to get up. I will send out for the doctor first thing in the morning. I would go now but cannot leave the children and I daren't risk taking them out in this cold." Esther nodded, she felt too tired to speak.

"I will take Dolly to the nursey and try to settle her, then I will come back with a cold cloth and some water. We will have you comfortable in no time."

In the nursery, Elsbeth changed the baby's sodden clothing and bedclothes. She wiped the child's face with a damp cloth and lay her back in the cot. Stroking the child's hair until, finally, she fell asleep. Still hot to touch, Elsbeth had no choice but to go to Esther. From the kitchen, she took a jug of water and some clean towels.

"Here we are dear, let's get you into some dry things." Helping the young woman into a dry nightdress she then sat her in the chair.
"Try to drink this. I am going to change your bedsheets then we shall get you back into bed."
Esther did as she was told without argument, she didn't have the energy to protest at the Mistress of the house waiting on her, it wasn't right, she thought, but she complied all the same. Once settled back into her bed, Esther sipped at the water, rolled over and fell asleep.
Elsbeth checked on the baby, Dolly was sleeping, her breathing laboured and deep. Her tiny face, still as red as a berry. Quickly she checked the other children, they seemed, thankfully unaffected by whatever this was.

The remainder of the night saw the woman making frequent trips up and down the stairs in the large house. The 2 affected slept, albeit fretful and laboured sleep. It was close to 5 in the morning when the stableboy arrived. He was surprised to see the lights on in the house, normally he had a good few hours alone before anyone in the house stirred. It was in the early hours that he did all of his stable work, cleaned the blocks and groomed the horses. He was a hard worker and would not stop until he was called into the kitchen for breakfast. It was a shock to him to be met on the steps by Mrs Stanhope. His initial thought was that she disapproved of his growing relationship with the housemaid, in which case he assumed he was for the high jump. Not a thing to get up this early for, surely?
"I need you to fetch the doctor, I have a note for you to take. I know it's early but he must come to the house as soon as he can."
"Yes, Ma'am. Is it the little one's?"
Elsbeth nodded.
"The baby, and Miss Esther, they're sick. Hurry, ask him to come soon. Take the buggy, you can bring him back in that if he's agreeable."

It seemed an age before the buggy could be seen coming back up the driveway. Elsbeth ran to the door to greet the doctor.

"I'm so sorry to have you up early Doctor, I left it as long as I could."

The middle-aged man looked tired as he entered the hall.

"You're not the first today, Mrs Stanhope. It appears we have an outbreak of influenza. I trust you are well?" Elsbeth nodded as she led him first to the nursery. Checking the baby over he sighed.

"She is struggling, have you managed to get any fluids down her?"

"A little, the last time I tried she brought it back up with the coughing. Will she be alright, Doctor?" Pulling a small bottle from his bag and placing it into Elsbeth's hand he shook his head.

"Difficult when they're so young, her with the start to life that she had. Keep her warm, try to make sure she drinks and give a drop of this every few hours. We have to hope her fever breaks soon. Where is the other patient? A housemaid I believe?"

"This way, Doctor. So it isn't the Typhoid fever?" The doctor shook his head.

"I doubt it, I hear there have been cases of Typhus further up the coast, can't say that I've seen any myself. The best we can do is keep the patients quiet and warm, if it is Typhoid, it will show itself to be soon enough."

Esther was soaked to her skin once again, she coughed, it was a weaker cough than previously, mainly due to her lack of energy. Elsbeth wiped her brow as she sat down beside her.

"How are you dear? The doctor has come to see you." Whispered the concerned woman.

"I'm going to listen to your breathing, my dear. Can you sit a little for me?" Esther could not, she seemed oblivious to the people in the room, oblivious to the stablehand that stood and stared from the doorway. The doctor continued to check the young woman as best he could. Eventually, he pulled the cover back over the shivering woman.

"Let us retire downstairs, give the girl some quiet and rest."

"Do I need medicine for Esther? Do I use the same one that you gave me for the baby?"
Elsbeth wanted to know.

"I am fairly certain the medicine will not help the girl, Mrs Stanhope. Her parents have been told of her sickness?"

"Not as yet, Doctor. I felt it wiser to get you here first."

Turning to the stablehand that had not left their side, the doctor talked quietly.

"Go to the Thompson house, boy. Fetch them here as soon as you can."

"Doctor?" Elsbeth was not liking the tone of his voice.

"The boy can take me into the village and bring the parents here on his return, is that agreeable to you Mrs Stanhope?"

"Of course, is it that serious Doctor?"

"I believe it is. Keep a close watch on the child, indeed I expect her to recover well as her fever has all but broken. Should the other children develop similar symptoms you can use the medicine that I gave to you. Warmth and liquids, Mrs Stanhope, it's all you can do. Come along boy, let's not waste time."

"What's happening here this morning? I've just seen the Doctor leaving like the devil was after him." Sally asked as she pushed the door shut behind her.

"We have a few cases of influenza in the house, Sally. Baby Dolly and Esther up to now. Esher is not doing well, the doctor has asked for her parents to be sent for as a matter of urgency." Sally flopped to the chair beside her, her mouth open.

"I shall need some help with the children this morning, the house is to be kept quiet. If I could leave that to you, I will tend to Esther and Dolly."

"Are you sure that's wise, Ma'am? I mean to say, won't do you any good to catch it. I could tend to them if you prefer?"

Elsbeth shook her head, she knew the woman meant well but it was her duty to tend them.

"Thank you, Sally. I shall be fine, the children ought to be awake soon. I am expecting the Thompson's anytime now. When they arrive, can you send them up to me?" Sally nodded. She set about preparing breakfast for the children, as usual, stopping only to let in the Thompson's.

"Just upstairs, Mrs Stanhope is expecting you." She smiled a softer smile than was the norm for her.

The Thompson's had all but 5 minutes with their daughter before she breathed her last uncomfortable breath. The room fell silent, a silence that drifted down through the whole of the house. Even the children as they ate their breakfast, stopped for a moment as though they knew. Elsbeth stood at the door and watched helplessly as the older woman sobbed into her daughter's still chest. The time stood still, nobody moving in that small, cosy room.

"Come along children, let's get our hats and coats on. It's cold but bright. Now, who would like to feed the chicken's?" Sally, biting back the tears, helped the younger ones with their coats. She had been asked to say nothing to the children. Elsbeth felt it best to tackle this conversation later. The Thompson's sat with Esther until the doctor came back. Now, they sat in the parlour with Elsbeth, staring into cups of tea. Elsbeth struggled with what to say, what could she say? Their lively, pretty girl had gone. In an instant, life had changed for them forever.

"Take as long as you need." Was all she could muster. She thought back to the time she lost her first husband, sure, there were many kind words uttered, none that helped in her grief and none that penetrated her mind. Tom came into her mind now, she knew it was an inappropriate time, yet she missed him now more than ever.

"I must check on the little one. I shall be back shortly, please stay a while."

Mrs Thompson gazed up at her, her eyes were red and swollen.

"Can I come with you?" A strange, yet simple request.

"Of course, dear."

The child was no longer red of face, her breathing less shallow than it had been during the night.

"Such a pretty thing." Whispered Mrs Thompson as she held the small hand in hers.

"I am so very, very sorry for your loss." Began Elsbeth, only to be met with the woman shaking her head.

"I know, dear. She was a bright one was our Esther. We weren't sure she would grow up at all, we dared to dream you see. She had a bad illness as a child, left her weak you see. The older she got, the more we thought that she would grow old, have children of her own. I think, He, had other idea's. We had her longer than we ever thought we would. We're grateful for that. She loved it here, you know? Made her happy in her way."

"Esther was a wonderful addition to our little family, the children will miss her dreadfully, as will we all."

"Oh, dear Lord, what a terrible thing to have happened. Do they know why?" Grace was stunned by what Mr Nash was telling her. Such a young girl too.

"Influenza, mind, it's been said she had a weakness of sorts that she picked up as a youngster."

"And the baby? How is baby Dolly? I must go over and see them, see if I can be of help."

"Doctor says the place is to be avoided until everyone gets the all-clear. Makes sense not to spread it, there's some that wouldn't fair well."

Grace agreed, she still felt she needed to do something to show their support.

"I'll speak to Milton, see if we can't offer some other help in the meantime. Good afternoon Mr Nash."

Making her way through the farmyard, Grace could see Mary brushing down the dogs.

"Hello, there Mary."

"Grace, how lovely to see you. How are you and the family?"

"Mary, we can't complain dear. Have you been to the hall today?"

Dusting down her skirts Mary got to her feet, the dogs running off into the house.

"Not today, I was planning on going over on Tuesday. Is everything alright?"

Mary headed for the farmhouse, gesturing to Grace to follow.

"Young Esther."

"The housemaid, the one that lived there? What of her? She hasn't run off with that stableboy, has she? I said to my Robert, there is a romance in the making if ever there was one."

Grace sat down as Mary poured tea for the pair.

"She has passed." Said Grace quietly.

"Passed where? I don't understand, Grace?"

"This morning, early, the poor girl has died, Mary." Mary sat down with a thud. She was confused. She only saw the girl day before yesterday, in the village with 3 of the children. No, Grace must surely be mistaken.

"Are we talking about the same person, Grace? You cannot possibly mean the young woman at the hall?"

"Yes, influenza so I heard. It was mercifully quick, her parents were with her, Elsbeth too and that young man you speak of. Terrible upset they all are, it's shocking, and her in her prime. I tell you, Mary, you never know the minute."

Mary sat and stared in disbelief.

"I must go over there, Elsbeth must be so upset."

"The doctor has advised against visiting for now until it's clear of the bug. Still, there must be something we can do?"

"Maybe we could offer help with the children, just until they find somebody else."

Robert entered the kitchen, pulling off his boots and reaching for a mug.

"Grace, what are you 2 cooking up?" He laughed. The look from Mary stopped his laugh cold. She explained the situation and the awful news.

"Oh, I am that sorry, I had no idea. Bonny lass she was too, such a waste and just overnight you say? Ain't right is it?"

"We were wondering what we could do to help, Grace tells me the doctor says no visitors for now. It's a bad lot this time of year, so many have gone down with it. Not often a youngster though."

"I don't want you getting it, Mary. I am all for helping where we can but, I couldn't bear for you to get sick." Mary patted his arm affectionately, she knew he meant it in the best way.

"I know dear, we must do something, I cannot sit here whilst poor Elsbeth is going through this."

"I shall talk with Milton, I'm sure he will agree with Robert but like you, Mary, I must do something."

The children took the loss badly, as was expected. They had grown fond of the funny, young woman in their time with her. She was the lighthearted one of the staff, in their young minds it brought back memories of their own parents and the realisation that nothing was certain. Mary had been the one to break the news to them, ignoring the advice of the doctor she had gone to the hall. The morning had been a strange one, with Elsbeth having the youngsters gather in the sitting room and every intention of telling them gently. It had not worked out that way, she attempted, in her mind to put words to that which she must say only to find that she could not. Mary's appearance at the door was a welcome one.

"I can't do it, Mary. They are so fragile, how am I to explain that which I do not fully understand myself?"

Mary put her motherly arms around the woman.

"Go to bed, dear. You look as though you haven't slept for a week. I shall handle this, I will be as careful and gentle as I can. It will do them no good if you run yourself into the ground, off you go."
Elsbeth did as Mary asked. Standing in the sitting room she held out her arms to the children.
"Come here children, let us all hold hands." The bemused children stood around the woman, clasping each other's hands until a circle was formed.
"Now, children. I have something very serious and important to talk to you about. No doubt you have all noticed a strange feeling in the house for the last few days? Miss Elsbeth has been a little more tired than usual and Sally has been looking after all of you by herself. This is because our dear friend Esther has gone to Heaven. Does anyone know what that means?"
William nodded his head.
"William?"
"It means that God has asked her to be an Angel, Miss Mary."
"That ain't right." Shouted David.
"Is too." Replied an indignant William.
"Miss Esther can't be an Angel, she isn't old enough." Protested David.
"William is correct. We will miss Esther deeply, but the Lord has another job for her to do. We have to be extra good for Miss Elsbeth as she is feeling very sad. Does this news make anyone else sad?"
The children nodded, Ruby began to cry.
"It's okay Ruby, my Ma is an Angel and she will look after Miss Esther." Comforted Jacob as he squeezed the young girls hand.
"We have to be strong now, as a family." Added Mary as she looked around the circle of sad faces.
"Will Dolly be an Angel too?" It was Doris that quietly asked the question.
"No dear, Dolly is feeling much better now."
This new information seemed to take a weight off Doris's shoulders, she smiled.
"Who will look after us?" added Martha. Mary shrugged, she wasn't sure what was going to happen in the coming weeks.
"Don't you worry about that my dear, there are plenty of people that will offer support until it is settled. You will all be in good hands."

News of young Esther's demise soon raced around the village, the overwhelming feeling was one of great sadness. Reverend Moore held a special service for Esther, it had been some years since the village had lost a local of such a young age and it hit hard. Friends of the girl read out touching stories of how they knew Esther, how she had touched their life. The Thompson's were visibly moved by the kindness bestowed upon them. The parents were distraught as they said a final goodbye to their eldest child.

Elsbeth and the children stood at the back of the church with Grace and Milton in the row before them. Milton was quiet, his mind often struggled with the loss of younger folk, a life half lived ended just like that. Grace held his hand, she knew to say nothing at times such as these.

The Thompson's normally noisy brood was unusually quiet, their red faces expressionless as they struggled to comprehend what had happened to their bossy sister.

The wake was not the normal lively affair that came after the parting of an older person with a life well-lived. Instead, it was sombre, short, with guests straining to leave the complete and utter sadness of the day.

Fourteen

The day was fast approaching and Grace could barely sit still. This was their only chance to bring their boy home and she could not sleep for all the 'what if's' that raced around in her mind. Billoughby rolled over for the second time that night to notice his wife was, again, not in the bed next to him. Pulling on his dressing gown and slippers he trudged once more down the stairs.

"Gracie, love. You must try to get some sleep. It'll do you no good to be too tired to make the trip." Grace shrugged, he was right, of course, he was. Still, she could not quieten her mind. Pushing the pot toward her husband she looked weary.

"I have tried, dear. I can't seem to stay asleep. What if he isn't there Milton? Then what?"

Milton poured the hot tea into a mug, shaking his head he had no answer. For the first time in a long time, the great Inspector Billoughby was stumped. He stared at his wife.

"All we can do is hope Gracie, other than that, well it's in the hands of the Almighty."

Finishing their tea the couple made their way back up the stairs.

Tom raced through his tasks that day. The innkeeper could barely keep up with the energetic young man.

"I don't know what you had to eat for your breakfast today fella, but I reckon I could do with a slice of whatever it was. You're getting through more in one morning than most could do in a week!" Tom smiled, as much as he felt a sense of sadness at leaving them in the lurch he wanted to be on that ship and away from the heartache that would not be settled until he was far away. The innkeeper's son was finding it hard to keep up with him.

"Slow down Stan, you're making me look bad." He laughed as the pair stacked the barrels in the cellar. What would ordinarily take most of the morning took merely a couple of hours. Lunchtime was busy as ever with tables to be cleared and ale to be served. It was during this time that Tom's ears picked up the conversation from the man in the suit, standing at the bar.

"No, fella. Nobody here by the name of Tom. You say he's in his twenties? We don't often get youngsters drinking in here, mostly regulars and they're all getting on. We get the odd fella's passing through, course we do. No one springs to mind. Here, hang on and I'll ask the missus and staff." The innkeeper walked to the end of the bar, calling his wife to him and muttering quietly, she shook her head.

"Stan, here Stan. Do you know of a Tom, fella there is looking for a missing lad name of Tom." Tom shook his head, his head that he was careful to keep low as he wiped the sop off the table. The innkeeper asked his son and the barman the same question.

"Sorry fella, can't help you there, none of the family or staff can help you there. Is the lad in trouble?"

The man shook his head. He would do, he wasn't about to say yes to that now was he? Thought Tom. The man ordered a pint and some food, he sat at the table and scribbled on some paper.

"Here, Stan. Take this over to that chappie." Tom placed the platter and mug on the table.

"Nice place your father has here."

"We think so." Replied Tom quietly. So, he assumed Tom was a member of the family, even better.

The Inn closed for the night, Tom sat back against his headrest on the bed. The ticket in his hand he wondered what his parents were doing now. He would write them, posting it before he boarded the ship. He set to putting down on paper what he could not tell them in person. There was a letter to Adam and Cate, one to Elsbeth and another to his parents. Sealing the envelopes he placed them on the side table and settled down for his last sleep at the Inn that had been so welcoming to him.

It was Wednesday morning, 10th April and the streets of Southampton were packed more than usual. Tom had stayed the night in a local inn, having spent the past days travelling to get to the dockside with plenty of time to spare. He did not want to miss this. He had left a letter for the innkeeper and family, thanking them for the chance they had given him, asking them not to think too badly of him. Tom explained briefly that he would be leaving on the great vessel, after all, who were they going to tell? He walked the crowded streets slowly, taking in all the sights and sounds, unaware that not a stone's throw away his parents were waking. Elsbeth was also waking up after a fitful night's sleep. She looked over at David, still curled up in a ball as he dreamt the dreams a child does. Elsbeth was certain that if Tom could only catch a glimpse of the boy, maybe, just maybe he would realise that everything was as it should be. Having broached the idea to the Inspector she was disappointed to find that he did not share her view.

"The lad has had enough upset over the months, no, Mrs Stanhope, I don't think it a wise choice to have him accompany us." That was all he would say on the matter, leaving Elsbeth with what seemed like no other option than to take him, herself.

It was 10 o'clock, Billoughby and Grace sat in the small room and ate breakfast with Grace nervously picking at the well-presented food.

"Try to eat something, love. It'll be a while before we get the chance to stop and eat." Coaxed by her husband. Grace placed a forkful in her mouth, she did not feel hungry but if it appeased her husband.

Elsbeth was taking no chances, she and David, dressed and fed, walked leisurely along the street. Elsbeth did not want to be rushing, she had not exactly told David why they were having this special treat away and the boy imagined it was a break for his charge after the upset of Esther. David was excited, not any of the boys from the village were lucky enough to see the Titanic off on its very first voyage, they would be green with envy when they found out. Checking her watch, Elsbeth saw that the time was marching on.

"Come along dearest, we should make our way to the dockside and find ourselves a good place to watch, it's nearly 11 o'clock."

Grace and Billoughby stood amongst the crowd, they tried to push closer but it was a battle.

"Over there, love. There's a better view of the top rails. My guess is, if he's here he will be at the rails." Grace kept a tight hold of her husband's hand as they made their way through the tightly packed gathering. They settled on a space and waited, neither one of them saying anything but their breathing heavy, lost in the noise of the crowd.

Elsbeth and David were making their way when the boy suddenly stopped, his face a beaming smile as he cried out.

"Captain Freddie, Captain Freddie, it's Captain Freddie Miss Elsbeth, LOOK!"

Freddie turned, he could have sworn he heard a voice calling him. He continued to walk toward the harbour when it came again, as clear as a bell.

"CAPTAIN FREDDIE!"

David pulled free from the hand of Elsbeth and sprinted toward the tall man. He was swooped up in a moment by the fisherman, his hug warm and genuine as he spun the boy around in his arms.

"Whatever are you doing here? Are you with someone, where are they?" David pointed to Elsbeth who had quickened her step to catch the boy up. Freddie smiled as she approached.

"Good to see you, Ma'am. Come to wave the ship off on her travels have you?"

"Something like that Captain. How are you? I must say, you were the last person I expected to see here today."

"It's a historic occasion, Ma'am. Couldn't let it pass and not be here, same with most of these." He waved his arms around the crowd, keeping the other tight around young David.

"Are you going on her Captain Freddie?" asked David.

"No son, too much money and too far a trip for old Freddie. I'm happy where I am young David. Now, have you been up close to her? I have a friend aboard, could get you a quick look-see before she sets off?"

Elsbeth's heart skipped a beat, could it be possible that he would do that for them?

Freddie placed David back on the ground.

"You get a grip of the Lady's hand youngster, don't want you going astray again now, do we?" David took Elsbeth's hand as he stared up at the man. It was so good to see him again.

"Could you really get us onboard?" she asked the man quietly.

"Aye, only for a minute, mind. Are you alright Ma'am?"

Elsbeth whispered into Freddie's ear, David strained to hear what was being said but it was far too loud with all of the people shouting and cheering around them. Freddie scratched his chin. Shame, he thought, she would have made him a perfect match. He had thought about her often since their meeting, still, who was he to stand in the way of greater things.

"Leave it with me, don't move from this spot and I'll be back as soon as I can."

The minutes ticked by slowly now. The gangway was a constant stream of people. Grace wondered how so many people would fit on the ship and be comfortable. Her eyes scanned the passengers as they waved from the rails, still no sign of her boy.

Tom was taking the ticket from his bag when the tap on his shoulder came. He half expected it to be the police, instead, the innkeeper's son stood there.

"I wanted to wish you luck Stan, I envy you this chance. Father will be so angry when he notices my absence but I had to come and see you off. Make yourself a great life, you deserve it." Tom was shocked, more so that the man had travelled so far to say goodbye in person. They had become quite good friends over the months, but this, this was strangely odd of the chap. Tom stretched out his hand, the man taking it in a soft grip.

"I'll miss you. Be safe. Write often and tell me of your new life?" Tom nodded as he looked at the sadness in the man's eyes.

"Ticket?" The man asked.

"Oh, yes. Here it is." Tom handed the ticket to the man at the rope. The innkeeper's son released his hand.

"Wait." Called Tom

Freddie returned to the pair that were patiently waiting.

"No can do I'm sorry to say. If we had been here earlier. I'm so sorry."

"You tried, thank you for that. I suppose we should find a place to watch the ship depart young man." Elsbeth's voice was shaky as she squeezed out the words to David. The trio moved forward as noon approached. They could see people lining the top decks of the great ship, waving flags and handkerchiefs at the crowds below.

Grace sobbed against her husband's overcoat. He wasn't here, they had made the journey for nothing.

"There my love. Maybe he changed his mind. He will find his way back to us I know it." Comforted Billoughby, his words lost in the noise.

As the enormous liner pulled away from the harbour there was more than one heart that was breaking in that moment.

Tom waved, his arm reaching high into the air. He contemplated his future and what he had given up. Finally, he lowered his arm as he pushed through people cheering and singing. The excitement of the day was vast. He smiled a little smile, this was it then!

"What do you think of that David? Do you imagine that one day you would like to set sail in a liner that size?" David shook his head, he liked the trawler, it was just big enough.

"No Captain Freddie, I don't think I would like to go too far away." Freddie was doing his best to keep the young boy occupied, mainly to distract the lad from the distraught sobs of Mrs Stanhope.

"What say you and I find our way to that pub on the main street and see if we can't get them to rustle us up a bite to eat?" He looked to Elsbeth as he spoke. She silently agreed with a nod. In all the continued merriment on the harbour, she felt numb, it swept over her like the mighty wave of a storm as she watched the tall man lead the child to a calmer place.

Billoughby took Grace by the arm, he knew it was hopeless to hang around any longer. The ship had sailed, most likely with their son aboard and there wasn't a thing they could do.

"Let's get you out of here my love." They walked quite a distance before they reached the street. The Inspector directed his wife into the inn, she had spoken no words since they turned their backs on the liner.

"Sit yourself down Gracie, I'll fetch a drop of something. Well, as I live and breath!"

"Hello, Mr Billoughby, did you come to watch the ship too?" David shouted across the room.

"We did that lad. Who are you with?" At that moment Freddie turned from making his order.

"Inspector, fancy seeing you here. Mrs Stanhope should be with us presently, she needs a moment. David, come over here, we can keep the Inspector and Mrs Billoughby company until the Missus returns."

Grace patted the boy's head, she was tired and wanted to go home. They sat making pleasantries in the inn for a good while. Billoughby looking at his pocket watch now and then. Eventually, he spoke.

"David, would you care to take a stroll with me, go see what's keeping Mrs Stanhope. I wouldn't want her to get lost." David jumped down from his seat, it was boring in here he thought and Miss Elsbeth did not know the place well.

"Wait here with my Gracie, could you Freddie?" Freddie nodded, he had been on his feet all day and the rest was a welcome one.

They walked the long walk back toward the harbour. David chattering away about how many people he had tried to count on the ship. He wondered where it would stop next, to which Billoughby explained it would stop off in France this very evening.

"I bet you can still see it if we get you up on my shoulders." He laughed to the child.

"You won't drop me, will you? I heard that if a person gets dropped on their head they are done for." Billoughby laughed, louder now.

He was a funny lad. Crouching down he held out his hand as he helped the boy onto his large shoulders.

"Ready?" He asked as he began to get to his feet.

"Ready." Called David, his voice a nervous, giddy shriek.

"Can you see it, lad?"

"I can too Mr Billoughby, it's all the way over there but I can see it." Came the excited reply.

Tom leant against the rail, if he didn't know better...No! This is what comes of not sleeping well, he thought. The figure got closer, even amongst the still large crowd he could spot that man a mile away. The figure stopped, it appeared the man was speaking with someone, a woman. He watched as the child was lifted from the shoulders and placed onto the ground, the woman turned to face the harbour.

Tom raced through the crowds, pushing his way to them, his eyes never leaving their frames. His steps were fast and steady. Elsbeth had the strangest feeling.

"Are you alright Mrs Stanhope? I'm sorry the trip wasn't a success, it was so kind of you to bring David and try to help us. I imagine we will... Elsbeth? Whatever is the matter?" She could feel something moving toward her. Elsbeth turned again as the arms swept her off the ground. She knew that touch, that kiss. Inspector Billoughby stood with his mouth wide open. That never was his Tom, was it? It was. Why on God's earth was he kissing Mrs Stanhope in that way and why was she letting him?

"I have missed you so much, my love." She whispered over and over.

Tom stepped back and looked at his Father, then David. It was all alright, everything was going to be just fine. Billoughby grabbed his son so tightly that Tom thought he would surely burst.

"Your Ma will be thrilled, oh, your Ma she is waiting for us. I don't know what we're going to tell her about, well, this?"

"For now, Pa. We'll say nothing." Replied his son as he took hold of his true love's hand.

Historic Events of 1912

1 January General Post Office takes over National Telephone Company

17 January British polar explorer Robert Falcon Scott and a team of four reach the South Pole to find that Roald Amundsen had beaten them to it

26 February–6 April National coal strike of 1912

16 March Lawrence Oates, a member of Scott's South Pole expedition leaves the tent saying, "I am just going outside and may be some time". He is never seen again

19 March minimum wage introduced for miners

29 March the remaining members of Scott's expedition die

30 March The University Boat Race on the Thames in London is abandoned after both crews sink.

11 April Irish Home Rule Bill introduced in the House of Commons, it fails to receive the support of the House of Lords

13 April The Royal Flying Corps is established by royal charter.

14/15 April The RMS Titanic sinks The White Star liner RMS Titanic hits an iceberg and sinks on her maiden voyage

22 April English aviator Denys Corbett Wilson completes the first aeroplane crossing of the Irish Sea, from Goodwick in Wales to Crane near Enniscorthy in Ireland.

May Liberal Unionist Party merges into the Conservative And Unionist Party.

2 May 3 July Board of Trade inquiry into the sinking of the RMS Titanic.

5 May 22 July Great Britain and Ireland compete at the Olympics in Stockholm and win 10 gold, 15 silver and 16 bronze medals.

13 May The Air Battalion Royal Engineers becomes the Military Wing of the Royal Flying Corps.

9 July Cadeby Main pit disaster: two underground explosions in the South Yorkshire Coalfield kill 91 miners.

15 July the National Insurance Act 1911 comes into force introducing National Insurance payments.

27 July Bonar Law, leader of the Conservative Party in opposition, makes a defiant speech at a massive Irish Unionist

rally at Blenheim Palace against Irish Home Rule implying support for armed resistance to it in Ulster.
August Cabinet ministers were accused of corruption in the Marconi scandal.
wettest British August on record
25–27 August the wet summer climaxes in a major rainstorm across England, causing floods mainly in Norfolk and Norwich
September Blackpool Illuminations begins
5 November establishment of the British Board of Film Censors.
12 November the bodies of Captain Scott and his team are found in the Antarctic
27 November concerted suffragette attacks on pillar boxes
18 December Piltdown Man, thought to be the fossilised remains of an unknown form of early human, presented to the Geological Society. In 1953 It is revealed to be a hoax

·

Printed in Great Britain
by Amazon

81066555R00102